W9-BAJ-150

AN AVALON MYSTERY

ENDANGERED
Eric C. Evans

Sam McKall is the campaign manager for United States Senator Maggie Hansen. When controversial environmentalist Steve Tate is murdered, the evidence mounts up against the senator's brother, Vernon Hansen. Vernon is a large rancher and outspoken opponent of the environmental movement whose cattle Tate had been shooting around the time he died.

As the investigation tightens around Vernon, Maggie's opponents are digging up her past. They want to link her to the murder and beat her in the election. Putting his own life in danger, Sam must stay one step ahead of the press to deal with political ramifications and solve the murder or see Maggie's career be destroyed.

Cover illustration by Ken Spencer
Cover design by Steve Monosson

ENDANGERED

•

ERIC C. EVANS

AVALON BOOKS
NEW YORK

PRINTED IN THE UNITED STATES OF AMERICA
ON ACID-FREE PAPER
BY HADDON CRAFTSMEN, BLOOMSBURG, PENNSYLVANIA

For
Myrtice and Charlie Evans
&
J.L. "Doc" and Eloise Sims
You were the sunshine of my spring

Chapter One

"**S**am, it's Smitty on line four," my secretary yelled from her desk in front of my office.

I took a few seconds to prepare myself . . . then picked up the phone.

"Sam McKall," I said.

"Sammy, this is Smitty." Wayne Smith was a reporter for the *Capitol Times* and the only person in the world who called me "Sammy."

"It's almost two. You're late." Talking with Smitty during a political campaign is like jumping into the ring with a heavyweight contender—if you are not on your toes, you're probably going to get KO'd.

"Any truth to all these rumors I'm hearing?" That was Smitty's way of making me nervous.

"I doubt it. What's the rumor today?"

"I hear that you guys had to refund some money to high-dollar contributors and that the FEC is planning an audit."

Earlier in the week we had received a couple of checks

1

from campaign contributors who had already given the legal maximum. Our accountant caught it and sent the checks back with our apologies. The mere mention of the Federal Election Commission would normally strike fear and loathing in the heart of any campaign manager, but I knew what he was talking about and it was nothing that would get the FEC's interest. But Smitty already knew that.

"Is that the best they could come up with?" I said. "They" were the Montgomery campaign.

"Well, did you take the money?"

"We had to return a few checks to people who had already contributed the legal maximum. But they were never deposited in our account," I said.

"Okay, it was weak. But you know, I've got to check out all of 'em," he said, laughing that he had wasted my time.

"You hear anything?" he added.

"Not really. I'm still waiting for your story on our Chamber of Commerce endorsement." Tracey Harmon came into my office and started pacing. She is the campaign press secretary and, almost without exception, she is as tough as nails. But even brave hearts tremble in fear when Smitty calls.

"Oh yeah, that's coming up right after my story on the sun coming up in the morning." We both laughed.

"How is this campaign shaping up compared with the last one?" Smitty asked in a slightly more serious tone.

"I'll tell you Smitty, it seems like every election gets more and more hectic. We're heading into what I call the sleep deprivation phase."

"You're worried about this one, I guess."

He was always putting words in my mouth—looking for a news angle.

"Not really. The Montgomery people are running an aggressive campaign but even in campaigns with huge leads, the last four weeks are always chaotic. And I usually only end up getting about four hours' sleep a night."

Smitty's reply was little more than a grunt and I could hear him thumbing through his notebook.

Smitty is the kind of reporter politicians hate, but campaign staffers secretly like. Some reporters will nail you to the wall without bothering to check the facts or even pretending to be balanced. Other reporters would not recognize news if Edward R. Murrow returned from the dead and handed them a story already typewritten and double-spaced. Not Smitty. He will take you to the mat, and it may be on a technicality, but he will have his facts straight and he knows how to make it hurt. But in the end he is fair and in this business that is all you can really ask for.

Smitty has worked the political beat for the *Capitol Times* since about the time Gutenberg invented movable type. I had never known him to be surprised or impressed by anything. He has seen it all—most of it with a cigarette and pen in one hand and a notebook in the other.

"I guess that's it," he finally said. "Call me if anything comes up." I have had literally thousands of conversations with Smitty and he has ended every one of them with the same request.

"You'll be the first I call," was my typical response even though, in most cases, nothing could be further from the truth.

I hung up and looked over at Tracey Harmon. I was glad the campaign was almost over, because she was wearing a hole in the carpet in front of my desk worrying about what Smitty was going to do to us.

"He doesn't have anything today," I said. The tightness in her face and shoulders immediately disappeared.

Tracey handled all the senator's media relations—except for Smitty. He is by far the most important journalist in this state. And Smitty liked me, so I handled him.

"Nothing?" she said. The corners of her mouth moved ever so slightly toward her high cheekbones.

"Nothing," I repeated.

"One of these days you are going to have to let me start taking his calls," she said, squinting her eyebrows together.

I laughed. "Just once I want you to tell me that before I take his call."

"I'll take 'em. Start sending him through to me," she said, folding her arms over her chest. Indignant.

Tracey is good—very good—and more than capable enough to handle Smitty, but it was better not to risk antagonizing him, and I had developed a rapport with him. And despite what she had just said, Tracey and I both agreed that it was best to give Smitty what he wanted whenever possible.

When Tracey left, I looked at my watch. Two o'clock on the nose. I reached over and turned up the radio sitting in my window seat. The radio in my office is always tuned to KFK—"all news all the time." The news was just beginning.

I listened to the first thirty seconds of the newscast and realized that the whole complexion of the campaign had changed.

"The body of Steve Tate has been found on a mesa overlooking a small canyon early this morning. Tate had been an outspoken advocate of stiffer enforcement of environmental laws, and the leader of a national environmental group known as the MountainLand Liberation Front. Tate had angered many longtime residents of Red Creek by advocating the listing of the yellow-backed minnow on the Endangered Species List. A move which many believed would give the U.S. Fish and Wildlife Service too much control over the region's main industries of cattle ranching and

mining. As yet, there has been no word from law enforcement authorities on any possible suspects. More
on this story as information becomes available.

At the state capitol today . . .''

The anchor continued on, but I did not hear a word she
was saying.

Chapter Two

When Maggie Hansen was first elected to the United States Senate a story like this would have been treated like any other murder. That was the early 1980s, when people considered environmentalists left-wing radicals and politicians in this state had regularly used them as whipping boys. A place to point the finger of blame. Not anymore.

In the mid 1980s the environmental movement was taken over by a group of more charismatic and politically astute leaders who dragged the movement—often kicking and screaming—into the mainstream of American politics. In the early 1980s politicians bragged about victories over environmentalists, but now politicians regularly argue about who is the most green and who has been greener longer.

This transition has caused considerable problems for politicians in states like Utah who were elected in one era, but now serve in another. Urban voters are now ahead of the environmental curve while most rural voters are still well behind it, seeing it as a threat to a way of life they cherish.

To win elections, Maggie has to get a significant number of votes from both the rural areas of the state and the "greener" suburban voters. That is no small trick. And getting progressively harder.

This murder would bring environmental issues into focus in a way which would be detrimental to Maggie's candidacy. Over the last several years we had gone through the painful process of repositioning Maggie's environmental stands. Where she used to be opposed to the environmental movement, we have gradually moved her to advocating carefully chosen and symbolic issues on both sides of the dividing line. It is what I call the we-can-have-it-both-ways position. We can protect the environment *and* our economic stability. This murder smoked out the inherent inconsistency in our positions, with the very real possibility of fracturing Maggie's voter coalition.

One of the most important strategic goals of any campaign is to control the campaign agenda. If a candidate can control what issues drive the election, that candidate will usually win. In this race the environment was a wedge issue that worked against us and for our opponent Jeff Montgomery. Therefore, we stayed away from it. We had forced Montgomery to talk about issues and positions that tended to solidify our support while eroding his. This murder would now turn those tables.

But that was not the end of the problems this murder presented to us. Red Creek is the senator's hometown. She left there to go to college and has lived in Wasatch City ever since, but most of her family still live in Red Creek. Her brother Leland is the county sheriff and another of her brothers, Vernon, is the area's largest rancher and an outspoken opponent of the environmentalists. Maggie's past positions on the environment and her connection with Red Creek have always made her attempts to become moderate politically suspect. Every slight modification of her environmental positions has been chronicled in the pages of the

Capitol Times. Like I said, it has been painful. And now all our work appeared to be teetering on a weakening precipice.

From the open door of my office I could see most of the campaign office. People on the telephone. Other people dashing from one desk to another, obviously under a dead-line. Volunteers stuffing the next mailer. More volunteers putting together lawn signs. Old pizza boxes on top of re-ally old pizza boxes. Dozens upon dozens of Diet Coke cans and half-empty coffee cups. And Maggie in her office on the phone.

I walked over to Maggie's office. She motioned for me to take one of the cheap chairs in front of her desk. I shut her office door and took a seat. She was holding the phone to her ear with her shoulder while playing with an earring she had removed so that she could listen more comfortably.

Maggie is a striking woman. Taller than most, and professional-looking. In a business suit, she would not look out of place in any boardroom in America. Dressed more casually, she looked like your typical grandmother on the way to a garden club meeting.

She had married young, had children young, and become a grandmother young. Both her father and grandfather had held elected offices. Her family had always been in-volved in state and local politics, so no one was surprised when Maggie announced she planned to run for the state legislature. But because she was challenging a powerful fourteen-year incumbent with strong political connections everywhere a politician needs political connections, people were surprised when she won.

Eight years later the youngest of her three children was almost in college and she was the Speaker of the State House of Representatives when one of the state's U.S. Sen-ate seats came open. Again people were not surprised when she decided to run, but this time no one was surprised at her victory.

That was eighteen years ago. Since then she rose quickly through the ranks of the United States Senate and was now the chairperson of the Senate Judiciary Committee. Maggie was approaching sixty-two years old and wanted to serve one more term.

"What's wrong?" Maggie asked as she hung up the phone.

I have got to work on my poker face.

"Steve Tate has been murdered," I said.

Maggie's face tightened immediately. The implications of the murder were not lost on her.

She sat speechless for ten or fifteen seconds, not moving a muscle.

"Murdered?" she finally said.

I nodded.

"By whom?"

"Don't know."

"How?"

"Don't know that either."

"What *do* you know?" She was about to switch into shoot-the-messenger mode.

"They just reported on KFK that he was murdered and his body was found outside Red Creek."

Just then my secretary Nina came in and told me Smitty was on the phone.

Maggie and I exchanged glances.

"Tell him I'll have to call him back," I said as pleasantly as I could. Now was not a good time to talk to Smitty.

"Let's get Leland on the phone," Maggie suggested after Nina had left.

He was not in the office nor did he answer his mobile. I suggested we call Vernon, thinking the details of the murder were undoubtedly all over Red Creek. She dialed the number.

"Hi, Vern—Maggie."

"Hey, Maggie. How's everything? You heard about Steve Tate?" Maggie had him on speakerphone.

"I'm fine. Yes, I have heard. What happened?"

"I guess he was shooting cattle on a little mesa up Sidewinder Canyon. Someone snuck up behind him and put a bullet in his head. I always knew it was him." I could hear the smile in his voice. Vernon and Steve Tate had been bitter foes.

"What do you mean, you always knew it was him?" Maggie said.

"You know. Shooting cattle. He always denied it, but I knew it was him. Everybody did," Vernon said, as if he had defied the odds and correctly picked the Super Bowl winner.

"Who killed him?" Maggie asked.

"Heck, Maggie, they just found him this morning. I doubt Leland has figured it out by now. I suppose they may never know."

"Vernon," Maggie said, "do yourself a favor and try to control your glee when other people ask you about this." She looked at me and shook her head as if to say "this is going to be bad."

"Ah, come on," Vernon said, "this is family. I know how to act, but I've lost over two hundred and fifty head of cattle to these whacked-out environmentalists. And I got to be honest, I'm having trouble working up a lot of sympathy. Look at what he's done—not just shooting cattle, but to this whole town. This whole part of the state. If he had his way, we'd all move up there with you guys and live in two-room apartments so that the rest of this state can be nice and pristine for when his East Coast buddies want to come hiking. I'm sorry he was murdered, but I am glad he is gone."

"Vernon." Maggie was talking slowly to add emphasis.

"Please—for your own sake and mine—do not ever repeat what you just said to anyone. That was way out of line."

"Gimme a little credit. I know how to handle myself. Like I said, this is family." His voice was growing more defensive with every syllable.

"Don't get mad, Vernon, I'm just trying to add a little perspective to this," Maggie said.

"I'm not mad, and don't worry, I'll tone it down," he said. But I could tell he was disgusted.

"Listen, keep me posted on what happens, and have Leland call me if you see him," Maggie said.

She hung up the phone and stared at it for at least twenty seconds.

Finally she looked at me and said, "Get down to Red Creek. We need to know how bad this is going to be."

Chapter Three

Before I left, I needed to prepare the staff for what might be coming. I called an impromptu staff meeting and briefed everyone on what had happened. There was some concern and I reassured everyone as best I could that things would be all right.

"I'll be back in a day or two," I said to close the meeting. "Any questions?" There were a couple. When would the printing be done on our next mailer? When was the new TV ad going up? As the meeting broke up, I asked Mike Turpin, my deputy campaign manager, and Tracey to stay behind.

We stayed seated while the others left the conference room, then Mike got up to shut the door.

"This is bad. Isn't it?" he said as soon as the door was shut.

"I'm not going to lie to you, Mike. It could be," I said. "But we can handle it. Maggie's brother Leland is still the county sheriff down there and we should be able to keep a pretty good handle on things through him."

Mike did not reply, but I could see the wheels spinning. I turned to Tracey.

"It'll take most of the reporters a day or two to start calling us for a comment."

She nodded.

"Here's what we tell 'em. First, no one talks to Maggie about this. Second, all we know is what we hear on the news. It's a major tragedy not only for Mr. Tate's family and the town of Red Creek, but the whole state. Steve Tate has enriched this state and helped carve out a heritage for our children we can all are proud of. Third, we hope whoever did this is brought to justice quickly. Got it?"

She nodded and asked, "What if they ask what we're going to do about it?"

"Just tell 'em we are not sure that there is anything we can do, but the senator will do anything she reasonably can to assist in the investigation."

"Has Smitty called yet?" Tracey asked.

"Yeah, but I had Nina take a message."

"How are you going to handle him?" I noticed without comment that she now seemed content to let me handle Smitty.

"That's pretty sticky. If I come out and deny that this thing will affect this race, the denial becomes a sidebar. *'Senator Hansen Denies Murder Will Affect Race,'* " I said, gesturing as though I were placing the headline at the top of a newspaper.

"Right, and of course that is all the story will be about. All the ways this murder will affect the race," she said.

"We've got to act as though the idea that this story could affect this race has never crossed our minds. Make them ask us about the possibility. Then we will have to put the stories off as long as we can, and give ourselves the best chance to put a better spin on it."

"Sounds good," she said. She made a few notes on the back of an old campaign brochure and left.

"Is this going to be all right?" asked Mike again after Tracey left.

"I'm sure it will be."

"What is the worst-case scenario?"

"Well, Mike, I guess Montgomery could use this to fracture our coalition and win the election. But we are not going to let that happen." I was using my voice inflection to make it sound as though I thought this was a long shot.

"Best case?"

"Same as it was fifteen minutes ago. We win."

Mike asked me questions for ten or fifteen minutes. We went over every possible scenario and I could see his trepidation gradually begin to ease. He realized that I was right. Yes, this was a problem, but there were ways to minimize the damage.

Until this murder, everything in the campaign had gone pretty much according to plan. There had been a few surprises, but nothing major. We had executed our strategy, stayed on message, and maintained a twelve- to eighteen-point lead depending on whose polls you believed.

I returned to my office and asked Nina to get me on the next flight to Red Creek.

She gave me a stack of messages at least an inch thick, and I immediately began returning the calls. It was almost five o'clock and most of the people I was calling had gone for the day. A lot of a campaign manager's time is taken up returning the calls of campaign contributors or volunteers who want to tell you how to run the campaign or tell you what a mistake you made by not taking their previous advice. One in a hundred of these calls provide me with something I can actually use. The others, while often amusing, are a waste of time. So when people are not in to take my call, it really makes my day. They feel like their input is important to me because I returned their call, and I don't have to listen to their bad ideas. At least one thing was going right.

At the bottom of the stack was Smitty's message. I looked at my watch; it was five-thirty. He would still be working, so I decided to wait until I got to Red Creek to return his call. That way I could give him the same treatment I give the contributors and volunteers—leave a message that I returned his call.

I was cleaning off my desk when Nina came and told me the 7:12 flight to Red Creek was full and the 10:30 had been canceled. Great. Now I was driving to Red Creek. Five hours down, five hours back. Nina suggested I rent a car to drive down. That way I could fly back. It was a good idea, so I had her make the arrangements.

I was cleaning my desk and making my final preparations to go out of town when Maggie came into my office. When Maggie is worried about something she comes to see you, otherwise you are summoned to her office. She sat on the sofa to the left of my desk with her legs crossed and her arms folded.

"What are we going to do about Smitty?" she said. I had worked for Maggie for most of the last thirteen years and I bet she has asked me that same question five hundred times.

"He'll nail us on this one," she added.

"Well, Maggie, he is in an interesting situation right now," I said, propping my feet on the desk and lacing my fingers behind my head.

"Yes . . . we're at his mercy," she said with an insincere chuckle.

"Not yet, not exactly," I said.

"How so?"

"We all know where this story is headed. But right now it is not a political story. It's a crime story."

Maggie was nodding slowly, her eyes intensely focused on me, waiting for me to explain.

"Montgomery and the media want this to be a campaign

issue, but neither one wants to be the first to link them. Montgomery wants the media to do it and the media wants the Montgomery campaign to do it. Meanwhile, Smitty will have to cover this thing like any other murder and Montgomery will have to be careful. The last thing he wants is to be accused of trying to benefit personally from it.''

''But this isn't just another murder. Steve was well known; everybody in the media knew him. And liked him,'' she said.

''That's true. They will have to cover it like any other celebrity murder. It is still a crime story. The fact that he was well known and had a political following will eventually lead the story from a murder to a campaign issue. Trust me—it will take some time for this story to mature from a crime into a symbol of a larger problem. When that process is complete it will land right in our laps, but until then Smitty has to bide his time.''

''Like a chained attack dog bides his time,'' she said, staring out the window behind my desk.

I laughed. So did Maggie, but like the chuckle, she didn't really mean it.

''It's really not much consolation. Instead of starting tomorrow, they'll start Wednesday or Thursday. So what?'' she said.

''Well, you're right. But it does give us a couple of days. Maybe Tate's girlfriend did it. Maybe he killed himself. Who knows what will happen in the next forty-eight hours.''

''I'd hate to know my political future hung on those chances.''

''You're right, but it does give us a little time to maneuver and prepare. It's better than catching this thing between the eyes first thing in the morning.''

''I suppose you're right.'' She sighed. ''But the worst part about going to the dentist is not actually sitting in the chair. It's anticipating the appointment.''

I told Maggie that I was going to have to drive to Red

Creek and asked her to set up a meeting for me with Leland first thing in the morning. She said she would, leaned over, gave me a reassuring pat on the knee, and left for her evening appointments.

I finished up at the office, left my desk clean, and drove home to pack. I am embarrassed to admit that the first thing I thought when I walked through the door was that I might need the cleaning service to come twice a week rather than once. Imagine a bachelor, living alone, needing a cleaning service twice a week.

While packing, I realized to what lows my housekeeping had sunk. I did not have any clean underwear. That was pathetic. Now I had to stop on my way out of town and buy some. That should bring me up to about eighty-five pairs of underwear.

I called Tracey at home. She wasn't there. I finally reached her at the campaign office.

"Hey, Tracey, sorry to bother you, but I need a ride out to the airport to rent a car and I figure we could use the time to go over a few things. Can you break away?

"No problem. Be there in twenty minutes."

She was there in fifteen and I was waiting by the curb all packed and ready to go—except for my underwear.

"Thanks for coming by," I said as I got in the car.

"Any excuse to get away from the office."

"Listen, there is a department store up here on the left; would you mind stopping there? I've got to run in and pick something up."

"Sure." She made the left turn and pulled into the parking lot.

"Just park on the curb in front and I'll run in."

"I don't mind walking in with you." *It's not a problem for you,* I thought.

We went in the store and I made small talk as I picked up a bunch of stuff I did not need hoping that she would find something that would distract her long enough for me to grab the underwear. It did not work. Finally, I went to the menswear department and picked up the underwear. I was not embarrassed to buy underwear, but when you are buying it on your way out of town, all the possible reasons, including mine, are embarrassing. But Tracey was merciful enough not to say anything even though I could tell she wanted to.

The rest of the trip to the airport was uneventful. I rented the car Nina had reserved for me, gave final instructions to Tracey, and was on my way to Red Creek. Within forty-five minutes I was out of the city and well into the countryside. Nothing can compare to the beauty of a fall sun setting over the Rocky Mountains. The way the fading sunlight attaches to the rustic autumn leaves makes them glow like the embers of a dying fire. I thought about returning Smitty's call but decided that he might still be working. Besides, how many sunsets like this do you get in a lifetime? So I drove in solitude until the sun slipped below the western horizon.

Chapter Four

Now it was eight-thirty and safe to call Smitty. I knew the situation Smitty was in—pulling hard against his chain, but unable to attack. He also understood my situation—standing just outside the reach of his chain, but unable to acknowledge his presence. For the next day or two we would both dance a rhetorical dance.

I dialed Smitty's number and waited for his voice mail. Smitty answered on the second ring.

"Newsroom. Smitty."

"Yeah, Smit, uh, Smitty, this is, uh, Sam McKall." I couldn't believe he was still at his desk. He must have absolutely no life.

Smitty chuckled. "You thought I'd be gone?"

"I figured you would, but things have been so hectic. You know, like I said earlier." A weak attempt to cover myself.

"Right. What do you know about this Tate thing?"

"You covering the crime beat now?" I danced.

"I'm just checking on a few things. Helping out. You know," he danced.

"Just helping out wherever you can, huh?"

"Something like that. Do you know anything?"

"What would I know?" I said as innocently as I could. "All I know is what I heard on the radio. You heard anything?"

"The usual stuff. High-profile murder, you know. You talked to Maggie about it?" he asked as casually as he could.

"We were both at the campaign office when the story broke. We had a brief conversation. Nothing of substance."

"What does she think?"

"The same thing everybody thinks. That it was senseless. A tragedy. A loss for Red Creek and the state," I said.

"Those two went toe-to-toe more than anybody I can think of," he said.

Tate and Maggie had fought many political battles, most of them very public.

"Well, we opposed Steve when we thought he was wrong and supported him when we thought he was right. Don't forget, if it had not been for Maggie we never would have gotten the expansion of the Jacob Mountain Wilderness Area that Steve was always advocating. Senator Hansen got that thing through the Senate while she was still in the minority." Most reporters did not realize how important Maggie's role in expanding that wilderness area had been, but Smitty knew it would not have happened without her. This is why we picked symbolic issues on both sides so that no matter what the situation we had something good in our record to point to. Reporters can and will always argue motive, but in politics, symbols are powerful things.

Although I could tell Smitty wanted to continue with this line of questioning, he couldn't without tacitly admitting he was working on a political angle. So he took a different tack.

"You talked to Sheriff Hansen today?"

"No." And now I was glad I had not. I hoped he did not ask about Vernon.

"You know how I can get in touch with him?"

"Creek County Courthouse, I guess."

"That much I got. I've been calling all afternoon and I can't track him down. You got a home number?"

"I am not at the office and I don't have it with me. Call Tracey and she can get it from the senator's Rolodex."

"Got it. How about Vernon?"

I decided to answer the question as if he were asking for the number and let him clarify. "Ask Tracey. I don't have it either."

It was a second or two before he responded, "All right. Call me if anything comes up."

"You'll be the first I call."

I pressed END on my phone and dialed Tracey's home number. She picked up on the third ring. There was music playing in the background.

"Tracey, this is Sam. Why didn't you tell me I was buying women's underwear today?"

"Well, uh—what?"

"I'm just kidding. Sorry to bother you at home. Am I catching you at a bad time?"

She laughed. "No. No, this is a good time." She put her hand over the phone, but I could still hear her say, "Mark, could you turn that down? This is my boss." I had never heard her refer to me as her "boss" before.

"You sure? I can call back," I said, trying to be accommodating.

"No, it's fine, really."

"I just talked to Smitty again."

"Really? How did he track you down?"

"I called him thinking he wouldn't be in and I could just leave a message that I returned his call."

"Oh. How did it go?"

"You want another drink?" I could hear Mark say in the background.

Tracey put her hand over the phone and said, "Sure, thanks."

"It went okay," I answered. I could picture Mark pouring the drinks and handing one to her. "He asked me about Tate. I stayed on message." That's what politicians say when they said what they were supposed to say.

"He also asked for Leland's and Vernon's numbers. I told him I didn't have them with me. I suggested he call you in the morning to get them."

"All right. Where can I get them? I don't have them either."

"Get them out of the Rolodex on Maggie's desk. But don't take his call first thing. Put off returning it until about one-thirty or two. Any longer than that and he'll get suspicious." I could hear the music come back up in the background. Mark was tired of the intrusion. I continued, "By then I will have talked to both of them and I'll tell them to wait until tomorrow to return his call."

"Okay. Got it."

"Listen, I'll let you get back to your guest. Sorry to bother you at home."

"Don't worry about it. This is important."

We finished the conversation and hung up.

I called Maggie to brief her on what had happened. She said that she had left word with Leland's wife for him to meet me at 6:30 A.M. at the Creek Side Café. Those Hansens are early risers. I had thought I might actually get five or six hours' sleep, but not anymore.

When I finally finished my calls it was well after nine. The night sky is never so beautiful as it was through the thin, clear air of the Rocky Mountains. But to really enjoy it in all its majesty, you must leave the city lights for the dark country roads. I was actually on an interstate, but that was close enough. The stars were big and bright, glistening in a million different directions and a million different places. Seeing the western sky is one of those experiences that don't keep very well. Each time you see it is like the first.

I arrived in Red Creek about 1:30 A.M., checked into the motel, left a 5:30 A.M. wake-up call, and went to bed.

Chapter Five

Even under perfect conditions I cannot sleep in hotel rooms, so the 5:30 A.M. wake-up call came as a relief. I dragged myself out of bed, pulled on a pair of jeans, T-shirt, and tennis shoes, and walked across the street to a convenience store. The weather was cool and pleasant, but I could tell it was going to be a hot day.

I bought a cup of coffee and copies of the *Capitol Times* and the *Red Creek Reporter*. As expected, both papers had front-page, above-the-fold stories on the murder. Also, as expected, Smitty did not write the story in the *Capitol Times*. The *Times* headline read: ENVIRONMENTALIST MURDERED IN RED CREEK, subhead: *Steve Tate had been outspoken advocate of protecting the yellow-back minnow.* A color picture of Steve standing at the mouth of a picturesque canyon accompanied the story. The *Red Creek Reporter* is a small-town newspaper and was about a tenth as thick as the *Times*. Its headline read: STEVE TATE MURDERED IN SIDEWINDER CANYON, subhead: *Hansen launches investigation.* Small pictures of both Leland and Steve accompanied the story.

I took both papers back to my motel and carefully read each story. There were no surprises. The known facts about the murder at press time had not changed significantly since the KFK story.

The *Reporter* had an interview with Leland. After Maggie's conversation with Vernon the day before, I was worried that Leland, like his brother, might not have the proper sensitivities. But Leland has been in elective office for over twenty-five years, so he knew how to handle a reporter's questions. I was relieved to be wrong.

"This isn't the Wild West. The days of settling differences with guns have been over for more than one hundred years. Mr. Tate's murderer will be brought to justice no matter who or what he is, and justice in this case should be expected sooner rather than later," was Leland's quote. And it was a great quote, although as a general rule I don't recommend putting deadlines on things with so many uncontrollable variables. But hey, Leland is the sheriff and it was his quote.

All in all both were good stories and like I predicted, there wasn't even a suggestion of any potential links to the campaign. I showered, dressed, and still had fifteen minutes before I was to meet Leland so I decided to call Tracey to see how the ten o'clock newscast went the night before.

I reached her at home.

"Hello," she said. I could tell I had awakened her.

"I'm sorry, Tracey, you asleep?"

"Yeah, but my alarm would have gone off in ten minutes. No biggie." She did not bother lying like most people do in the same situation.

"What was the ten o'clock news like last night? I was still on the road," I said.

"Nothing new, really. Three stations had it as the first story; one station had it second. They were all anchor voice-overs. Channel 7 did a separate story on the debate tomorrow night, but they didn't talk about the murder.'' I was expecting that they would do a debate story because they are hosting the debate.

"I'm going to fly back up tonight," I said. "Make sure we don't accept any appointments for Maggie tomorrow. She needs to relax and do some debate prep, and nothing else. She does better at these things if she is rested, so make sure nothing goes on the schedule without clearing it with me first—unless Maggie puts it on, of course.''

"Okay. I'll make sure they don't. How's it going down there?''

"Not much happening yet. The papers weren't too bad either. I'll fax up the *Red Creek Reporter* story after I'm done with Leland. I'm going to meet him in a few minutes.''

"Good. Anything else?'' she asked.

"No, I don't think so. Oh yeah. Could you pick me up at the airport tonight?

"Sure. What time?''

"I'm not sure yet; check with Nina this afternoon and she'll know.''

We finished the phone call and I headed for the Creek Side Café to meet Leland. When I walked out of my hotel again at 6:25 A.M. it was already seventy-five degrees. The summer heat in Red Creek is unbearable for those who aren't used to it, but this was October. By late fall it usually becomes livable and the winters there are downright gorgeous. Highs in the 70s, lows in the 50s. But mid-October it can still be hot and it was.

As I walked the three blocks from my hotel to the café, I noticed how much Red Creek was changing. It had been two years since I had last been there. Four or five new condominium projects were in various stages of construction and quaint little coffee shops and restaurants that tourists like had popped up all over town.

Red Creek had been "discovered" not only by the environmentalists but also by tourists and retirees too. This place was changing and changing fast. In a few years it would be unrecognizable as the Red Creek I had always known. The area around Red Creek is known for its beautiful red rocks, sheer cliffs, breathtaking canyons, and is host to three national parks, all within reasonable driving distance.

The Creek Side Café was an institution in Red Creek. The building itself was built in the 1940s and the café opened in the 1950s, and from what I could tell, had never been remodeled. There would be no tourists in there, just locals.

I eat at the Creek Side every time I come to Red Creek because the food is irresistible. I'm a 90s kind of a guy and I watch my diet—fruits and vegetables, some fish and chicken along the way, and every now and then a steak. But you have to make exceptions for certain things, and the Creek Side Café is one of those things. Pancakes, waffles, eggs, hash browns, biscuits, bacon, and sausage are the breakfast fare at the Creek Side. Heart attack on a plate, but lick-the-plate-clean delicious. Order a fruit plate and a latte and all you'll get is contempt from the waitress and laughter from anyone who hears you order. The Creek Side Café is my guilty pleasure.

Leland was already seated and sipping a cup of black coffee when I arrived. He is about five or six years younger than Maggie, about six foot two with a small potbelly. He always has a ready smile and a knee-slapping laugh. And even though he is the sheriff I have never once seen him in any kind of uniform unless you count Justin boots and Wrangler jeans. But the single most distinctive thing about Leland Hansen is his left arm. It's missing from about four inches below his elbow. I think he lost it in a hay bailer during the 1960s sometime.

He greeted me like I was one of the family. We gave our orders to Wilma, who has been the waitress at Creek Side for as long as anybody can remember. I have always enjoyed watching her work. She doesn't really serve the food to you as much as she throws the plate and food at you in such a way that the food lands on the plate in front of you. It tops anything I've ever seen on David Letterman's Stupid Human Tricks.

"Well, you didn't come all the way down here to catch me up on the United States Senate," Leland said as Wilma threw us our food. "This Tate murder got you a little nervous?"

"I'm more than a little nervous." Leland was one of the most savvy politicians I knew and completely devoted to his sister, so I did not mind laying it all out with him.

"Me too," he said.

"Any leads?"

"Two," he said, holding up two fingers in case I couldn't hear through the wad of pancakes in his mouth.

"Can you tell me about them?" I was digging into a short stack of pancakes that were melting into pieces almost before they hit my tongue. I wished I could eat like this all the time.

"I'll tell you, but this goes no further," he said.

"No problem."

"Tate had been involved with a young woman half his age. She moved out or he kicked her out—I don't know which—about three weeks ago. Apparently, they made a pretty big scene when it happened. Yelling and screaming at each other out in the yard and stuff. I'm told they were throwin' clothes and furniture out doors and windows. I guess the neighbors were used to a lot of disturbance because no one called us. There's not any kind of report, but a lot of witnesses.''

"Have you talked to her?'' See, my girlfriend theory wasn't so far-fetched after all.

"No, that's the thing. She's gone. She was staying at a little motel here in town, but checked out the day before yesterday. And I can't find anybody who knows where she is. We'll track her down and see what her story is.''

"How long do you think that'll take?'' I said.

"Who knows. If she didn't do it, my guess is that she won't be too hard to find. Few phones calls, that kinda thing.''

"You said you had two leads,'' I said, with a fork full of hash browns in one hand and a link of sausage in the other. There was not much of a premium for manners at the Creek Side.

"Yeah, this is probably the best thing we got right now. About six months ago Steve was on one of these radio talk shows. Runnin' his mouth like he always did. Wilderness Act this, Endangered Species Act that. Well, they started taking calls and one of the callers came on and said, 'Steve Tate, we know where you live, and you're gonna die.' Click. Hung up. In his normal fashion Steve let a string of obscenities fly and the station cut to a commercial. Well, the station had that caller ID. They identified the number and called me. I found out the address and the number. It was at one of the bunkhouses out on Vernon's ranch. Vernon laughed and got a big kick out of it, but said I could go out there and look around. I was kicking around out there, going through the motions. I mean, I thought it was just a crank call but I just happened to lift the lid on this ol'boy's footlocker and in the corner I could see this galvanized cap. Like the ones that go on the end of a threaded pipe. Sure enough, it was a homemade bomb.

"It belonged to this cowboy by the name of Jones, Ty Jones. I waited for him to come in for supper and I arrested him and hauled him down to the jail. I knew Ty and his family before this because I had arrested his brother for assault about two years ago. He's still doin' time at the state prison. Anyways, we never could prove who made the call to the station. But the county attorney cut a deal with him, first-degree misdemeanor on the bomb charge, dropped the other charges, and he did three months. He's still around, but he doesn't work for Vernon no more.''

"What do you think, anything to either one of those?''

"It's hard to say. I wouldn't be surprised if either one of them did it or if neither one of them did it.

"I got two pieces of evidence," he said, slicing open a fried egg and letting runny yolk run onto a piece of toast. "Whoever killed him either followed him up Sidewinder Canyon or just happened upon his car—about a mile and a half from where he was eventually murdered. Then took the same trail to the top of the mesa Steve took and shot him. The state crime lab will be able to determine what kind of tires left the tracks.

"The other solid piece of evidence is the bullet. It went in but it didn't come out." Leland stopped eating long enough to see if I would be squeamish thinking about the bullet lodged in Tate's head.

"The ballistics on that'll tell us a lot," he continued. "What kind of gun, how far away, that kind of stuff.''

"How'd you find the body?''

"Somebody called that same station. And said, 'Steve Tate is dead up in Sidewinder Canyon.' This time whoever called used a pay phone at a grocery store.''

"You said this Jones guy was stupid, but no one is that stupid. Are they?''

" 'Bout half the people I arrest are that stupid.'' He laughed.

"It seems like Jones is your man," I said.

"He's at the jail right now drying out. One of my deputies picked him up at one of those taverns on the south end of town near the Nevada border, .25 blood alcohol content and strung out on meth. I'm gonna go over and talk to him as soon as he comes to this morning. I got him on suicide watch. Right now he don't even know he's in jail," Leland said.

"I would think that lead looks pretty good,"

"It's a good start. We really couldn't prove anything the first time. Everything we had was circumstantial. Ray—you know Ray Hajek, the county attorney—kind of bluffed him into taking the deal. Otherwise, he might've beat the whole darn thing. Who knows what we'll end up with here."

I had finished my breakfast and the guilt was starting to set in when Leland noticed Vernon coming in and waved him over to our table. I hadn't seen Vernon for at least six years. He was only a couple of years older than Maggie was, but he made those two look like ten. A lifetime of cigarette smoke and desert sun had taken their toll on Vernon.

"I thought I might find you here," Vernon yelled as he hung his cowboy hat on the rack by the door. He came over and sat down on Leland's side of the booth.

"Wilma, get me a short stack with a side of bacon and coffee and, oh yeah, some of that low-cal butter." That is the Red Creek answer to a Big Mac, large fries, and a Diet Coke.

"Sam, I haven't seen you in a while. What brings you to town? Steve Tate?"

"Pretty much," I said as I straightened the sugar packets.

"Vernon, why didn't you tell me those were your cows Tate was shooting when he got killed?"

That was the first I had heard of it.

"I just found out last night. Thought you knew anyways."

"How would I know where your stock is grazing?"

"I don't see what it matters. You got Ty in jail, what else do you want?"

"Oh, come on, Vernon, we don't have anything on him. He's been passed out drunk since before I called you last night. Hadn't said word. I had three reporters ask me yesterday whose cattle those were. And I told them I didn't know. How is it going to look now when it comes out that they're yours? Ain't gonna look good."

"I had this same conversation with Maggie yesterday. You people need to back way off." He gave me a sharp look. "At first I didn't know they were mine. I got over fourteen thousand head of cattle. Do you think I know where all of 'em are all the time? At least six different ranchers use that canyon to get to their grazing leases. By the time I found out, you called and told me about Ty. Then all I could think of was calling his mother, that poor woman. She's already got one son up at the state prison, you know," he said to me.

"All right, all right." Leland held his hand up as if to say, "You're right. I'm sorry." "I'm just trying to protect our rear ends on this thing. We don't need it to be worse than it has to be."

Managing Vernon was going to be a problem, I could see that.

"While I'm thinking about it, gimme the names of everybody else who has cattle up that canyon." Vernon, surprised, complied, and Leland wrote down the names.

"Why should these people matter?" Vernon said as Wilma threw his food to him.

"Whoever killed Tate either followed him out there or happened upon him. I'm making a list of people who had a reason to be out there. And people with cattle up there got a reason to be up there."

"And a motive." Did I say that out loud? Both men were staring at me. I guess I did.

"He's right. They got a motive. And if they were up the

canyon Sunday night they might have had an opportunity,''
Leland said.

"Darn it, Leland, you got Ty already. How much more
are the rest of us going to be drug through?'' Vernon said,
dropping his fork and folding his arms over his chest.

"I am going to conduct a professional investigation,''
Leland said, leaning forward and pointing his index finger
up and down on the table as if he were pushing a button
over and over again. "I'm going to follow every lead and
check out every story until I find someone I can charge
with this murder.''

"Well, then, I guess you'll be investigating me?''

"Not just you, anybody who had a reason to be up there.
I can't talk to everybody but you. Don't you see that? These
newspapers would come down on us like a ton of bricks.''

"Yeah, I see,'' Vernon said. He pushed the rest of his
breakfast away to illustrate that he had lost his appetite,
and left the café without another word.

Leland just stared at Vernon as he left and shook his
head. When he was gone he said, "This ain't gonna be
easy. I know everybody on this list.'' He pointed to the list
of ranchers Vernon had named. "I grew up with 'em, went
to school with 'em. Look, here's Jack Meters.'' He pointed
to his name. "I go huntin' up at his cabin every year. His
wife and mine are always doin' things together.''

"Maybe when this Jones guy wakes up, you'll have all
the evidence you need.''

"Let's hope.'' He pointed to the list again. "The longer
guys like this stay in the mix, the uglier this thing is going
to be.''

Chapter Six

I needed a place to make some phone calls and send a few faxes, so Leland offered me a desk at his office. He drove me to my hotel. I picked up my rental car and followed him to the sheriff's office.

Leland's offices were in what is known in Red Creek as the Old Courthouse. In the mid-1970s the city fathers decided it was time to build a new courthouse and update Red Creek's image. Leland, who had only recently been elected sheriff, hated the idea and refused to move into a new building.

The Old Courthouse had been built during the 1930s at the height of the Depression, and the story behind how it was built had become part of Utah's political folklore and helped create the mystique of the Hansen family. Maggie had told me this story at least a dozen times.

She would say:

The Eighteenth Amendment to the Constitution calls for popular election of United States senators. Before that amendment was passed, U.S. senators were elected by state legislatures. But in the early 1900s, many states went to "Senatorial Primaries" to elect senators. In effect, candidates for U.S. Senate stood for election in a "primary" and whichever candidate won the primary was then elected by the state's legislature.

During the last senatorial election in Utah before the Eighteenth Amendment took effect, a three-term incumbent by the name of Robert Haley was seeking reelection and being challenged by Jackson Smith, a political newcomer. Smith had been a railroad executive and was a very energetic and charismatic fellow. He worked extremely hard and made the race close—a lot closer than people thought that it would be. But in the end, Haley won by less than six hundred votes.

On election night Smith conceded the election to Haley and soon resumed his job at the railroad. But about three weeks before the legislature was to convene, the county clerk from Haley's home county killed himself—shot himself in the head. At his desk he left a rambling note apologizing to Smith for what he had done, and saying he could not live with himself. Even though the letter didn't explain what he had done, most people assumed he had rigged the election for Haley. But no one could ever prove it. However, the allegation itself was enough to get the Smith people working again.

At first they made a few discreet inquiries of key legislators and found that there was some support for ignoring the results of the elections and electing Smith. As you can imagine, the Haley people fought back with a vengeance and the battle was on. Who could call in the most favors? Who could twist the most arms? Who could make the most deals?

Dad had been elected to his first term in the legislature during the same election that featured the Senatorial Primary. But even though he was a political newcomer, he had more innate political skills the day he was elected than most politicians at the end of their career. He could count votes, or as he called it, "count tickets," and he could see that the vote was going to be close. He knew his vote was going to be important, maybe even pivotal. He also knew that the longer he waited to make his deal, the better the deal was going to be. So he just sat in Red Creek and waited for the legislature to convene. When the day came, most legislators had committed one way or another and the vote appeared to be tied. Rep. Hansen from Red Creek would decide who the next U.S. senator from the state of Utah would be. The state nearly came to a standstill waiting for Dad to say how he planned to vote. Every paper in the state had stories about Dad, the Rancher from Red Creek—kingmaker. On the night before the legislative session was to begin, he sent a message for Smith to meet him at the hotel where he was staying.

When Smith arrived they chatted for a minute or two across a small table about one thing, then another. Then, from his briefcase, Dad pulled a sheet of paper that had only three letters typed on it—IOU—and handed it to Smith.

"If you sign that, you have my vote," he said, "and you'll be a United States senator. If not, I'll vote for Haley and he'll win."

Smith simply nodded. He wanted to hear more.

"From time to time as U.S. senator, you and I will have dealings together," Dad continued. "You'll need a favor from me, or I'll need a favor from you. There will be the normal give and take. I'll help you where I can and I hope you'll do the same. It's up to you. But this debt won't be repaid until I give this IOU to you and ask for a favor."

Smith picked up the paper and studied it for a minute or two, weighing his options.

"Two conditions," Smith said.

"They are?" Dad asked.

"Number one, I will not do anything illegal."

"Nor would I ask for such a favor," Dad replied.

"Number two, when the time comes you have to present the IOU. It can't be done through an intermediary."

"Done."

The deal was made and Smith was elected to the United States Senate—by a one-vote majority. And to Smith's credit, he never forgot the deal he'd made. And Dad held the IOU for over sixteen years.

By the time 1932 rolled around Smith had a seat on the Senate Appropriations Committee and Dad was the Speaker of the State House of Representatives. They were now two very powerful men. Meanwhile, the Depression had tightened its grip on Red Creek. Most of the ranchers in town had lost their ranches and the mines on the south end of town were shut down. Things were desperate. In the fall of 1933 Dad took a train back to Washington and cashed in his IOU.

He wanted federal money for a new courthouse in Red Creek and the money to pave Main Street. Senator Smith went to work and got three quarters of the money needed. Dad got the rest of the money from the state legislature. To make a long story short, they named the street after Senator Smith—Jackson Street— and the Courthouse after Dad—the Willard Hansen Courthouse.

So when they started talking about moving the sheriff's office out of the Old Courthouse, Leland steadfastly refused to move. Finally they cut a deal with him. The new courthouse would be built and the Old Courthouse would be renovated for office space. But instead of relocating all the county offices to the new building, the sheriff's department would be the main tenant of the Old Courthouse. Leland took the deal and they built a new courthouse. The new courthouse is a nice building and fits in with the older architectural style of Red Creek, but it cannot match the Old Courthouse with its brown sandstone complete with bell tower and the sixty-year-old oak and maple trees that surround it.

When we pulled into the rear parking lot I could see a small cluster of reporters waiting by the door that Leland usually uses. It looked like three or four print reporters and a TV reporter sent down from Wasatch City. I didn't recognize any of the print reporters, but I knew the TV reporter. He was John Mayfield of Channel 7 News. But nobody I knew referred to him by his given name. Everybody simply called him Hardcopy. He's never seen a story he couldn't sensationalize.

As soon as the reporters spotted Leland walking toward the door, they dashed over to meet him. The camerawoman who was with Hardcopy scrambled to get the camera on and focused. I parked in the rear of the parking lot and walked up only close enough to hear what they were asking Leland. Leland stopped a few feet in front of the steps to the door to take their questions.

"Is Tyson Jones under arrest for the murder of Steve Tate?" Hardcopy said as he shoved his way to the front of the pack and stuck a microphone in Leland's face.

"I'm doing fine, thank you for asking," Leland said, and flashed them his trademark smile. The print reporters had a little chuckle, but Hardcopy just looked perturbed.

"No," Leland said, "Mr. Jones is under arrest for drunk and disorderly conduct, possession of a controlled substance, and violating the terms of his parole."

"What is he on parole for?" asked one of the print reporters.

"Can't remember the exact charge, but had to do with the bomb."

"How long did he serve on that conviction?"

"About three months, I believe," Leland said as he scratched under his hat.

"Is he a suspect in the murder of Mr. Tate?" Hardcopy said.

"Not officially. No one has talked to him since the murder."

"He's been in your jail for over twelve hours, sir. When do you think you might get around to it?" Hardcopy said. Reporters do that righteous indignation thing so well.

Leland just looked at him as if he were a puppy who just learned to beg. "He was passed out when my deputies brought him in last night and hasn't woke up yet. But when he does, me and Barney are going right over to talk to him."

"Barney who?" said Hardcopy, preparing to write down the name while still holding the microphone.

"Barney Fife, my deputy. F-I-F-E. I've also given him permission to put his bullet in his gun until this case is solved." Hardcopy had written down the entire name before he realized what the other reporters were laughing at. I swear I saw smoke coming out of his ears.

"I'm sorry," said Leland, using his one good hand to give Hardcopy a good-natured slap on the back. "When he wakes up and is coherent we will question him and make an assessment at that time."

"You say officially he is not yet a suspect. What about unofficially?" said a voice I recognized.

"Let me be clear on that first part, Randy." Oh yeah, Randy Fox from the *Red Creek Reporter*. I had never met him, but talked to him on the phone many times. "I said he was not an official suspect and I don't know if he ever will be. As for your question, I am not going to speculate on who may or may not be unofficial suspects at this point. Or even if there are any.''

"Okay, are you going to question Ty Jones about the murder?'' said Hardcopy. Apparently he had not had enough.

Leland just smiled and said, "I'll refer you to my previous answer.''

"Sheriff, hasn't Jones threatened to kill Steve Tate before?'' one of the print reporters said.

"There were allegations, but Mr. Jones was never charged with or tried on those allegations,'' said Leland.

"Why not?'' asked Hardcopy.

"The same reason you weren't.'' A truly puzzled look crossed Hardcopy's face until Leland added, "No proof beyond a reasonable doubt that he did it.''

"What were the circumstances of those allegations?'' asked the another reporter.

"All I'm going to say is that there were allegations which we investigated. I turned the results of that investigation over to Ray Hajek, the county attorney, who decided against charging him,'' said Leland. Then added, "I agreed completely with his decision.''

"At the time did you believe Jones had made the threats?''

"I was never sure who made the threat and neither was Ray.''

"Was this the incident with the radio station?'' asked another print reporter.

"It was.''

"And that investigation yielded the bomb charges?''

"That's right.''

"Anyone else charged in connection with the bomb or the threat?''

"No, there wasn't.''

"What is Ty Jones's brother in prison for?" Hardcopy said.

"Thomas Jones was arrested and convicted of assault about two years ago. He is two years into a five- to fifteen-year sentence." Leland did not look at Hardcopy as he replied.

"Who was the victim in that case?" Hardcopy said.

"You'll have to get that information from somewhere else."

"Didn't you arrest him?" asked Hardcopy.

"Yes."

"And you don't remember?"

"I remember, but it has no bearing on this case. If you want that information you can look it up yourself. I assume you are able to do some research," Leland said, his eyes boring in on Hardcopy.

"Leland, didn't Ty work for Vernon? I mean when that bomb incident happened?" asked Randy.

"Yes," said Leland.

"Who's Vernon?" said Hardcopy.

"He's the sheriff's brother," said Randy while writing in his pad. Hardcopy just smiled.

Nothing was said for a few seconds while the reporters were examining their notes, making sure they had asked all their questions.

"Is that it?" Leland said.

The reporters nodded while still making notes and Leland went inside. I waited a minute or two until the reporters had dispersed and followed him in.

Most politicians want you to critique their performances with reporters and I was expecting Leland to ask my opinion on how he did. But he did not ask. Nevertheless, I thought he had done a great job. He answered their questions honestly and straightforwardly and did not allow them to put words in his mouth. I have always admired Leland's political skills but the fact that he did not need me to validate them only made me like him more.

He put me in a small office just down the hall from his and not far from the fax machine. I called Maggie to brief her on what I had learned so far.

"Maggie, I've got to say I am more than a little worried about Vernon. He seems out of control," I said.

"I know what you mean. He has always been out of control. I swear, half of what he says is said purely for shock value," she said. I could hear the frustration in her voice.

"I think you need to call and talk to him. Leland tried to this morning and he got mad and stormed out of the Creek Side," I said.

"I don't know where his hot temper comes from. It certainly was not from my mother or father. Both of them were very even-tempered. My dad could get mad and carry a grudge, but he never flew off the handle like Vernon does," she said.

"I don't know about all that," I said. "But Vernon is a loose cannon. We need a strategy for how we are going to manage him. And we need it pretty soon. Leland had a little impromptu press conference out by the Old Courthouse. One of the reporters asked about Vernon and Ty Jones. Hardcopy got this huge grin on his face. I'm sure he is trying to track him down right now," I said.

"I'll call him as soon as we hang up, and plead with him to tone it down," she said.

"The best thing he could do is avoid doing any media interviews, especially with Hardcopy."

"Right. I'll suggest that to him. But you know how they are, especially Hardcopy. If you keep turning them down, they'll just ambush you," she said.

She asked how Leland's press conference went. I told her how well he had done and asked her to get Tracey and

Mike on the phone for me. She put me on hold and a few seconds later they had me on the speakerphone.

I briefed both of them on what was going on.

"Have you already given Vernon's number to Smitty?" I asked Tracey.

"No. He called and left a message, but I haven't returned it. And by the way, I called information just to see if it was listed. His residence is unlisted but there are two listings for his ranch. So it won't be that hard to track him down. Not for Smitty," she said.

I thought about it a few seconds, then said, "Call him back right now and give him all of Leland's numbers, home, mobile, everything. If he asks for Vernon's, tell him you'll have to call him back. I'll go in and make sure Leland takes his call. He's great with the media. Maybe if he talks to Leland he won't want to talk to Vernon."

Mike had several questions about the next set of mailers we were going to try to get out. He seemed to have everything functioning smoothly.

I hung up and walked into Leland's office. He was on the phone with the jail.

"Considering his condition last night, he might not wake up for several more hours," Leland said into the phone.

There was a pause while the other person was talking. Leland propped the phone between his ear and shoulder and motioned me to take a seat in front of his desk.

"That's right. Has the doctor been in there again this morning?" he said.

Pause.

Leland kept a neat desk. I suspected it was neat because he did not do much paperwork.

"Good. Call me the minute he wakes up."

Short pause.

"No, just let him wake up on his own."

Pause.

"We'll talk to you then. Good-bye."

He hung up and looked over at me.

"Has Wayne Smith called you today?" I said.

Leland laughed. "You mean Smitty? Yeah, he called twice yesterday and twice already this morning. I was just getting ready to call him."

"Good. He's been asking us for Vernon's number. I hope if he talks to you he won't want to talk to Vernon."

"Vernon loves to see his name in print. Reporters around here know who to call to get the good quotes. He has said some outrageous things." Leland laughed.

I wasn't quite so amused. I could feel the muscles in my back and neck tighten, and a pit opened in my stomach.

"During my last election," Leland continued, "Vernon was quoted in the *Red Creek Reporter* as saying that my opponent would rather 'eat dirt than have a real job.' "

I laughed, but even while I was doing it I could feel the pit in my stomach getting larger.

"Why don't I call Smitty right now while you're here? I'll put him on speaker," he said, and started fishing around on his desk to find Smitty's phone number. I gave him the number from memory and he dialed.

"Newsroom," said a voice I did not recognize.

"Wayne Smith, please," said Leland.

Then, without another word, we were put on hold. I love newsroom etiquette. A few seconds later Smitty picked up.

Smitty asked most of the same questions that the other reporters asked. Then said, "I understand the cattle Tate was shooting were your brother's."

"That's right."

"Is that confirmed? I understand you didn't know whose cattle they were yesterday," Smitty said.

"That's right. At least six ranchers use that canyon to get to their leases, so it could have been any one of 'em."

"And you did or didn't know your brother was one of the six?"

" 'Course I knew. But I didn't have any way of knowing

whose cattle of the six were actually in the canyon that night.''

"I see. You said something about leases?"

"Yeah, ninety-three percent of the land in this county is owned by the federal government. In order to graze cattle we have to lease the grazing rights from the federal government," Leland said.

"And Vernon and five other people own leases that are accessed through that canyon? What's it called? Sidewinder Canyon?"

"Yeah, Sidewinder. I'm not sure of the exact number of people who have leases up there, but that's about right."

"Who are the other five?"

"I don't have a confirmed list yet; I can send it to you when I do."

"And this Jones guy, he used to work for Vernon."

"That's right."

"Do you know how I can get in touch with Vernon?" See what a political mastermind I am?

"I don't know where he is today, but here is the number out to his office—"

"I think I already got that number," said Smitty, and read a number.

"That's it," Leland said.

"I haven't been able to reach him there. Do you have his home number?"

I knew Leland well enough to know that he realized not giving the number now would simply appear evasive and just delay the inevitable. Leland understood that the last thing you should do in a situation like ours is damage or destroy your credibility with the media. So he gave Smitty the number.

"Okay. I think that'll do it. Call me if anything comes up," Smitty said.

"Don't count on it," Leland said with a chuckle. I guess that's another approach.

I went back to the office I was using, clipped the story from the *Reporter,* and faxed it to Tracey. I then called our campaign pollster and media consultant. Our pollster was based in Wasatch City, but was in Washington, D.C., on business. And our media consultant lived in D.C. It was getting close to 10:00 A.M., which was almost noon on the East Coast. I needed to call them before they left for lunch. In Washington, the only thing that rivals the importance of the lunch hour is the cocktail hour. In my experience both were so long that they often overlap in the middle of the afternoon. Washington is funny that way. The earliest most people get to work is 10:00 A.M.; lunch is at noon and goes to about 2:00 P.M. The cocktail and dinner hours begin at roughly five o'clock and stretch into 10:00 or 11:00 P.M. When people first arrive in Washington this type of work-day seems terribly inefficient. But those who have what it takes to make it in that town quickly learn that all these lunches, cocktail hours, and dinner parties are where the real work of Washington is done. Office hours are kept simply to push the paper and validate what was agreed to at yesterday's cocktail party. So the best time to call some-one in D.C. is between the hours of 10:00 AM. and noon; otherwise it will likely be the next day before your call is returned.

I called the pollster first. We were scheduled to begin a poll tomorrow night and I felt like the timing would be better after this story had a few more days to germinate. Going with the poll as it was scheduled would have only created a false sense of security because enough people had not heard about the murder, and for those who had, it was simply a murder to which the political connections had not been made. In order to get an accurate understanding of the mood of the electorate, we needed to wait for a couple of more days. I briefed him on the problem, and like any good pollster, he panicked. I talked him in from the ledge and asked him to fax me a draft of the questionnaire we were planning to use. Clearly, some of the questions needed to be changed.

I then called our media consultants. TV guys are in many ways the alter egos of pollsters; nothing scares them—as long as you have enough money to "fix" the problem. Or in other words if you have enough money to buy a never-ending barrage of TV ads, nothing worries them. We had been expecting that at some time during this campaign we would have to answer an environmental attack from the Montgomery campaign. So we had been preparing a possible ad to answer those attacks. I had done the first draft of an ad script, so we had a place to begin. I asked him to rewrite what I had done and to get the new copy to me as soon as possible.

By the time I had gotten off the phone with our media consultant, Leland's receptionist had already brought in the questionnaire faxed to me by the pollster. I was reading it over, writing new questions and making changes to old ones, when Leland stuck his head in my office.

"Ty's awake. Want to go over with me?"

Chapter Seven

The Creek County jail was more like an old hospital than a jail. It was a cold, antiseptic place with few windows and lit only by fluorescent light. The interview room was small and adorned by a metal table, two chairs, and a two-way mirror. Ty Jones sat in one of the metal chairs with his hands handcuffed behind his back. I was sitting in the next room watching through the two-way mirror with the county attorney Ray Hajek seated next to me and one of Leland's deputies leaning against the wall next to the two-way mirror.

Ty looked a lot older than I had expected. His skin was a pasty-pale shade of white, there was a mix of old and new bruises on his arms and ankles, and his hair was long and bushy. He appeared to be asleep, with his chin resting on his chest and his eyes closed. Leland opened the door to the room we were in and asked if we were ready. We were. He closed our door and in a second he walked into the interview room.

Leland's entrance startled Ty from his nap. His eyes were bloodshot and swollen. He looked around the room for a second or two with a panicked look in his eye. Then just as suddenly, he realized where he was and relaxed as if he were in his own living room.

"Leland, what the heck's going on?" he said after his composure was fully recovered.

Leland walked around behind Ty without saying anything and unlocked his handcuffs. As Ty rubbed his wrists, I could see what looked like needle tracks on his arm. Leland took his seat at the other side of the table and turned on a tape recorder, which was in the middle of the table between the two men.

"Ty Jones, you are under arrest . . ." Leland read him his Miranda rights. "Now, do you want to have an attorney present?"

"That depends," Ty said, leaning back in his chair and putting his feet on the table in front of him.

"On what?" Leland said, almost but not quite concealing his contempt.

"On what the heck's going on. That's what," Ty said.

"Okay, I'll tell you what, I'll ask some questions, and if I come to one you think you ought to talk to a lawyer about, we'll stop. Sound reasonable?"

"Can I smoke?"

"I don't care."

"Don't got no cigarettes."

Leland stared at Ty for a few seconds, shaking his head. Finally without a word he got up and walked out of the room. After he was gone, Ty got up and walked around the room, stopping right in front of the two-way mirror and staring in at us as if he could see right through it.

"I wanted so bad to charge him with attempted murder or conspiracy or some kind of felony," Ray said to no one in particular. I guessed he was talking about the previous incident with the bomb and the radio station.

Leland walked back in with a pack of cigarettes and a small box of matches under his arm. Ty let us know that he knew we were there by waving at the mirror. I noticed that the fingers of one hand had the letters H,A,T, and E tattooed on each of them respectively. He stared at us for another moment and then sat back down at the table. He opened the new pack of cigarettes, tore the filter off one, and lit it. He took a long, deep drag, then blew the smoke in Leland's direction.

"All right, I'm ready," he said, and put his feet back up on the table, crossing his arms over his chest.

"Can you tell me what you were doing Monday afternoon and night?" Leland said.

"Before I answer that, what am I in here for again?"

"Possession of a controlled substance, drunk and disorderly, and parole violations," Leland said.

Jones shrugged his shoulders and said, "Okay, what about Monday?"

"What were you doing that afternoon and evening?"

"Sleeping, I guess,"

"Where?"

"In the back of my truck."

"Where?"

"I think it was just off that road that goes out to the old sawmill."

"Do you live in your truck now?"

"What's it to you?"

"I'll take that as a yes," Leland said. He hesitated for a second to see if Jones would correct him. He didn't.

"Sleeping or passed out?" said Leland.

"What's the difference?" said Jones.

"I don't suppose there is much of a difference to you," Leland said. Jones just laughed. "Was anybody with you?"

"No."

"Can anybody confirm where you were?"

"That's one I'll have to think about," he said.

"What did you do earlier in that day?"

"In the morning, I went to my job."

"Where is that?"

"I sweep and mop the floors and clean the bathrooms at Herbie's," Jones said. Herbie's is a bar on the south end of Red Creek that caters to a clientele much like Jones himself.

"How long have you been working there?" Leland said.

" 'Bout two months."

"What did you do after that?"

"Started drinking, I suppose. Is that a crime these days?"

"Where were you drinking? At Herbie's?"

"Sometimes I just trade out with Herbie."

"Is that what you did on Monday?"

"Maybe, can't remember."

"Kind of a will-work-for-liquor routine, is that it?"

"I guess that's pretty much the way it works out," Ty said. He hadn't stopped smiling yet.

"Ty, when is the last time you saw Steve Tate?" Leland said.

He stopped smiling and tipped his chair back down on all four legs. "Okay. I want to talk to a lawyer."

I spent the afternoon trying to work on the poll and a script for a new TV ad, but could not concentrate. I kept thinking about Ty Jones and what he had told Leland. There were several different ways to interpret almost everything he had said and how he had acted. In some ways, maybe in a lot of ways, Ty Jones is stupid. But years of experience have made him very wise to the criminal process. He had not only avoided saying anything that would incriminate him, but he had also left himself quite a bit of room to fabricate whatever story he needed to in order to protect himself.

On one hand, the insolent attitude toward Leland and the nonchalant way he had accepted being under arrest would make one think he was unaware there had been murder and he was a suspect. I had so little exposure to anything like this, I still believed that guilty people acted guilty. I considered this generalization and decided that like most generalizations it was probably wrong.

On the other hand, perhaps Jones covered his feelings of guilt with a cross between aggressive behavior and a devil-may-care attitude. I had noticed that he left room to create an alibi for the time of the murder should he ever need one, and he carefully avoided saying what he had been doing at the time of the murder.

Or perhaps he was so arrogant and stupid that he thought that the body had not been discovered.

I looked at my watch and decided I had better call Maggie and tell her what I had learned so far.

"Look, Sam," she said, still a little irritated at me, "there is more to this story than the murder. The reason I wanted you to go down there was to get a larger understanding of what's happening in Red Creek. If I wanted to know about the murder I could've just called Leland."

"What do you suggest I do?" I said.

"We both know that I haven't always agreed with what the environmentalists are doing down there. I've fought them more often than not. And frankly, I haven't always been right. You know that. But I have been involved in enough of these issues to know that the media is going to be biased in the direction of their opinions. I want to know what the environmentalists are saying. That's what is going to find its way into print." She was right. I had been worried about Vernon, but he was only one of several wild cards in this thing.

"Do you know Omar Blackford?" she said.

"I know of him, of course, but I've never met him," I said.

"Omar is an old family friend; his father and my father were very close," she said. "Omar is very proud of his position as father of the Red Creek environmental movement, but he's reasonable. I've always been able to work with him. That's why I want you to go meet with him. He can give you a balanced view from the enviros' perspective. I also talked to Larry Klinger, the U.S. Fish and Wildlife Service's man on the ground down there. He has agreed to give you a detailed briefing on what's going on with the yellow-backed minnow. He is also expecting your call.''

I jotted down their names and numbers.

"Now, I don't know Klinger that well," she continued, "but Omar Blackford lives about fifteen miles north of Red Creek, in a little area known as Gunlock. Ask Leland for the directions.

"When Omar's father died—I can't recall his first name—he was the largest private landowner in Creek County. I'm not sure but I think Omar owns the largest ranch in Creek County," she said.

"He still operates a ranch?" I could not believe it.

"Oh no, he doesn't operate it. When their parents died, Omar's two sisters took their shares of the family fortune and moved to the West Coast, leaving Omar with his share of the money and the ranch. Not long after that, Omar became interested in the environmental movement. He devoted his life to it. Until then he'd kept the ranch going, more out of a sense of duty than the need for money. In fact, I bet he was losing money on the ranch.

"Anyway, he closed down all of the ranching operations and turned the entire ranch into a nature preserve. And not only did he shut down his ranch, he didn't allow any cattle grazing or hunting on his land and he only allowed catch-and-release fishing on the creeks and streams that ran through his property.

"People were okay with that, but what made people really angry is that he kept buying his federal grazing permits every year so that no one else could use them. That's why

Vernon hates him so much. I am sure he would like to get his hands on Omar's leases,'' she said.

''Vernon can't be the only one who doesn't like Omar,'' I said.

''No, Omar's enemies have been mounting for years. At first when he started all his protesting people just thought of him as a harmless eccentric. He wrote a regular column for the *Capitol Times*. But his ideas were so far out of vogue, people just laughed at him and didn't worry too much about it.''

''I'll bet that all changed when some of these national environmental groups began to take notice of what was going on in Red Creek,'' I said.

''Well, yes and no. People were mad at Omar for stirring things up, but once Steve Tate showed up he got most of the attention. You see, by the time Steve had moved to Red Creek and kind of taken over as the de facto leader of the environmentalists, Omar had kind of faded into the background. My guess is this murder will push Omar back out in front again, and frankly speaking, that's not all bad,'' she said.

Maggie had a few more questions about Vernon and this girl from Denver. I told her what I knew. We finished our call and I made arrangements to go meet Omar Blackford and Larry Klinger.

I did what I could on the TV script and the poll questionnaire and walked back into Leland's office. He was standing with his back to his desk looking out his window. When he heard me come in he took his seat behind his desk.

''I talked to Tate's girlfriend,'' he said.

''When?''

''Finished about two minutes before you walked in here,'' he said.

''Who is she?''

"She's a girl by the name of Watts, Sharon Watts."

"How is she?"

"Uh, she broke down in tears when I told her Tate had been murdered. Then she got hysterical when I told her I needed to ask her a few questions."

"Really? What do you make of that?"

"It's really hard to say. It's easier to make judgments when you're talking face-to-face with someone." He shrugged his shoulder to reinforce the idea that he didn't know what to think.

"Anyway, she was pitching a fit and hollerin,' then her dad came on the phone. I introduced myself and told him why I was calling. Then he got mad too. I apologized, but told him I needed to talk to his daughter and the best thing he could do was just bring her back to Red Creek so I could ask her a few questions. He told me I would be hearing from his lawyers and hung up. You know, that's one thing I enjoy about this job—talking with big-city lawyers."

"Where is she from?" I said.

"Denver. Sounded like pretty well-to-do people too. Most people who say you'll hear from their lawyers have never even been in a lawyer's office. But not this guy—he sounded like the kind of man who had two or three lawyers sitting around his office in case he needed to send somebody out for sandwiches."

"What's next?" I asked.

"Wait to hear from her lawyers, I guess."

"What can you tell me about Larry Klinger?" I said.

"Larry Klinger is a good man. If it weren't for him I would not be able to keep the peace over this minnow thing." He paused for a second, then added, "Well, I wouldn't have been able to keep it as long as I did anyway."

"How so?" I said.

"He's a greeny, no doubt. But he is reasonable and insists on following the processes outlined by law. And the environmentalists know they need him on their side to get what they want, so they have to listen to what he says. The way it's worked so far is I have handled the ranchers and he has handled the enviros—as far as keeping everybody under control. Couldn't do it without Larry.''

''Where is he from?'' I asked.

''I don't know much about his personal life. He came here from Wasatch City, but I don't think that's where he is from originally. He lives a few blocks from here with his wife and a couple of kids.''

''Have you talked to Vernon today?'' I said.

''No, I've left several messages for him at every one of his numbers. He's ignoring me. After seeing the look on that reporter's face today when he found out he was my brother, I imagine the next time we'll hear from him might be on the six o'clock news.''

I had been in denial of it all day long, but unfortunately I had a gut feeling he was right.

Chapter Eight

At least ten miles off the road to Omar's ranch was a dirt-and-gravel road that gave my poor rental car fits, but I found the place without too much trouble. It was a brick colonial-style home that looked completely out of place sitting there in the middle of nowhere. It had its own charm, with tall white columns in front and a beautiful flower bed in the center of a circular driveway made of a large gravel that crunched under my feet as I made my way to the front door.

I knocked on the big oak door and waited. And waited. I was about to leave, thinking that he must not be in, when he finally answered the door. He was at least two inches taller than me, with a lean athletic build and long graying hair pulled back into a ponytail.

"Hello, Mr. Blackford, I'm Sam McKall. We spoke earlier on the phone?"

"Oh, Sam," he said, and stuck his hand out to shake mine. "How are you? It's good to meet you."

57

"Thank you for taking the time to meet with me," I said.

"I'm glad to do it," he said. And I could tell by his smile he was.

He took me into a large family room with a big over-stuffed sofa and two wing chairs. He sat in one of the wing chairs and motioned for me to sit on the sofa.

"Maggie, ah, Senator Hansen says you need a little background on what's going on down here," he said after we had exchanged small talk for a few minutes.

"That's right. I know a little bit about all the controversy but not nearly enough. And with this murder I'm afraid it is going to be a major issue we'll have to deal with," I said.

"Yes, I'm sure it will be," he said as a smile crept into his eyes and I could tell that the idea of Maggie scrambling to explain her environmental position was not entirely un-appealing to Omar.

"I guess all the controversy started with the yellow-backed minnow," I said.

"There are a lot of environmental issues down here, un-protected wilderness, vanishing wetlands, wild and scenic rivers, and even other endangered species. But no question the yellow-backed minnow is by far the hottest issue right now."

"How come?"

"I've been working on these issues for over twenty years. When I first started I was a lonely voice down here. No one listened to me, at least not in this state. In fact I was dismissed as some kind of nut. But gradually things started to change, at least at a national level.

"At first the environmental movement was just a radical fringe, a bunch of hippies talking about things no one cared about. We did a lot of talking and protesting but nothing got done. But about fifteen years ago the public opinion on these issues began—ever so slightly—to shift in our favor.

Gradually we grew in prominence to the point that we were seen as a voter group to be courted and cultivated.

"We managed to find new, more charismatic, less abrasive and confrontational leaders. And slowly the green movement began to build momentum. Now it is one of the most potent political forces in the country. Don't you agree?" His smile was now in full bloom.

"Oh yes, yes I do," I said. I wouldn't be in his living room were it not the case.

"As the movement began to pick up momentum we were finally able to get environmentally friendly legislation out of the Congress. The Endangered Species Act, the Wilderness Act, the Wetlands Act, Wild and Scenic Rivers Act.

"Of course, those bills aren't perfect, but they have proven to be semi-effective tools. It took us a while to learn how to use them, but we have. And people around here haven't liked it.

"First, we came at them with the Wilderness Act. We identified all the land we could in the region that met the criteria to be wilderness. We fought for legislation to protect it. We have had some success, including the Jacob Mountain Range that Maggie, I mean the senator, helped us on. But we haven't been able to get the rest of it done. It is impossible to do without any help from the other members of Congress from Utah. We had Maggie helping on the Jacob Mountains and we barely got that done.

"But the Endangered Species Act is different. It doesn't require an act of Congress. It is administered by rules and regs," he continued.

"What you're saying is there is a process already in place you can use without any further involvement by Congress?" I said.

"That's right. About eight years ago, I noticed that other groups around the country were having a lot of success with having species listed on the Endangered Species List. So I started looking into it. It turns out that it is almost as ef-

fective as controlling development and protecting the environment as the Wilderness Act, and in some ways more
effective.''

"How so?'' I said.

"There is only one way to protect a species from going
extinct, and that is to protect its habitat. That means you
clamp down on anything that alters or destroys the habitat
used by that particular species. Get it? No development in
habitat. The law is clear. None. And in most cases the absence of development equals protection of the environ-
ments. So not only do you protect the species but the land,
the water, the air, the river, stream and creek banks, everything. The whole ecosystem. Whether it is wilderness or
not,'' he said. His smile was nothing less than triumphant.

"So the Endangered Species Act became your weapon
of choice?'' I said.

"Well, tool of choice anyway. The other acts are important and they are being used effectively in other places
around the country. But here in Red Creek the Endangered
Species Act seems to be the ticket. The yellow-backed minnow is poised to be our first major success.''

"How did the yellow-backed minnow ever come into
play?'' I asked. I had always been aware of what was going
on in Red Creek and knew that there had been a major
battle over the yellow-backed minnow and the Endangered
Species Act. But that was the extent of my knowledge.
Maggie had been right; I needed to know this stuff and I
needed to hear more than just the ranchers' side of it.

"That's an interesting question. It's been a long time
since anyone has asked me about it.'' He laced his fingers
behind his head and leaned back in his chair. "About seven
years ago, I had been studying the Endangered Species Act.
You know, finding out how it works, where you go, what
you do to get the process started. That kind of thing. During
that time, my sister got divorced down in LA. Although
she didn't say much about it, I could tell it was messy. She

asked if she could come and stay with me for a while. While she was here we pulled out all the old family albums. There were thousands of pictures, and in one of them I am tending to a fishbowl full of these minnows and my sister said to me, 'Remember, Omar, how you used to keep an aquarium full of those little minnows?'

"I didn't think much about it until later that night. She was in bed and I was back to studying the Act. Then it dawned on me. When I was a child those little minnows were everywhere. They were in every river, every creek, every lake, and every pond. But now you can't find them. I hired a group of environmental consultants in California to come in and do a study of these fish and they reported that this was a species of fish unique to this area and that its numbers were dwindling. They said it was a good candidate for listing on the Endangered Species List. So you see, all this was started by little ol' me.

"But when I first started talking about yellow-backed minnow and the Endangered Species Act, people around here thought I was crazy, and I wasn't making much headway. I knew how the process worked, but I didn't know *whom* to work to make the process work. You know what I mean?"

"You didn't understand the politics," I said.

"So I wrote a few letters to a few friends of mine around the country who had done this before. They sent me tips and suggestions. Before long the U.S. Fish and Wildlife Service started taking me seriously. Then Steve Tate showed up in town.

"I mean he just showed up one day on my doorstep like you did today, except unannounced. He told me he wanted to help me list the yellow-backed minnow and that he knew how to do it. He told me that some of our mutual friends had suggested that he come out and help.

"He took things over and formed a group called the MountainLand and Liberation Front. Stupid name, don't you think? It reminded me of the old radical days when no one listened to us and nothing got done.

"Anyway, Steve just took things over. He raised the money from back east. You can't imagine the kind of money it takes to work this process. It takes lawyers keeping the pressure on the court, money to hire biologists to keep the U.S. Fish and Wildlife honest. A lot of stuff like that. And he raised it.

"But Steve had a flaw or a blind spot or whatever you want to call it. I guess you could say it turned out to be a fatal flaw. At first, when we were trying to draw attention to what we were doing down here, his flamboyant, in-your-face styled served a purpose. But lately, in the last year or two his style was getting in the way of our ultimate goal. In a way, *he* was becoming the issue, not the environment, not saving the yellow-back minnow.

"And he just reveled in throwing our success in the face of the locals. I mean he just lived for it. When you're working with the locals here you can't always be in their face threatening legal action against them and laughing at them every time you win a victory or get closer to listing. It's counterproductive in so many ways.

"Then there was the matter of shooting the cattle. I had always suspected, as did everybody, I suppose, that it was Steve and his crowd out there shooting those cows. I confronted him about it several times, but every time I did, he would just deny it. In fact at one point, he and the MountainLand Liberation Front offered a five-thousand-dollar reward for information leading to the arrest of whoever was shooting those cattle. I thought it was a sham at the time, and as things turned out it was.

"So, rest his soul, having Steve around was a mixed blessing. I warned him on many occasions that he needed to tone it down, that one of these days one of these cowboys was going to reach his breaking point." Omar was shaking his finger at me as if he were warning me. I felt a little awkward. He continued, "But Steve would just slap me on the back and say, 'Don't worry, OB'—that's what he called me—'I know what I'm doing.' "

Omar leaned forward in his chair and shook his head. He was done talking, and telling this story had to be a cathartic experience for him. I sensed that he felt a little guilt for the way Steve had died and thought that maybe the warnings he gave to me were the ones he wished he had given to his friend. But he just sat there staring out the window of his library for what seemed to be two or three minutes.

"I'm sorry for your loss, Mr. Blackford," I finally said.

"I am sure everyone will miss Steve, but we'll just have to keep going. I guess a lot of Steve's responsibilities will now fall to me," he said. His eyes looked blank and distant.

"I'm sure you will be just as effective as Steve would have been," I said.

"In some ways I have to be more effective than Steve; we are just at the crucial stages now," he said, his eyes focusing on me for the first time since he finished talking about Steve.

"You can handle it, Mr. Blackford," I said.

"Please, call me Omar."

Omar showed me around the rest of his house and ranch. It was a beautiful spread that stretched for miles in every direction from his house. I envied Omar. Not many lives offer you the freedom to pursue whatever you desire. Most of us have to deal with the day-to-day vagaries of life. Namely, providing food, clothing, and shelter. And many of those who aren't troubled with those concerns end up wasting their lives in a frivolous search of pleasure.

I didn't see eye to eye with Omar on some issues, but I did admire him for devoting his life to a cause that was bigger than mere self-gratification and attempting to leave the world a better place. I wished him luck and left to go meet with Larry Klinger at the U.S. Fish and Wildlife office.

The U.S. Fish and Wildlife Service had converted an old convenience store into an office. I went through the front door and was greeted by the receptionist who spoke with a heavy New York accent. I gave her my name and told her I was here to meet with Mr. Klinger. Yes, he was expecting me. She showed me back through a small maze of cubicles to a small office with a lot of maps and colored pins on the wall. The receptionist pointed me toward Larry's office and then left without saying another word.

Larry was working at his desk. He was a man of average height and build with dark hair and a closely cut beard. He wore a uniform comprised of khaki shorts and long-sleeved shirt, which Larry wore rolled up past his elbows, and hiking boots.

"Larry, I'm Sam McKall," I said.

"Sam, it is very nice to meet you. After so many phone conversations over the years it is nice to put a face with a name," he said as he got up from his desk to shake my hand. He had a very firm handshake and he grabbed my elbow with his left hand as we shook.

I had always enjoyed talking to Larry on the phone; he was always easy to work with and was reasonable in his approach to his job. Leland and Maggie both had told me how much they liked having Larry around.

"I'm sorry to say that I haven't been paying as much attention to your problems here in Red Creek as I should have over the last few years. But I have taken a crash course today. I'm just coming from Omar Blackford's place," I said, taking the only other seat in his office.

"This is a real tragedy, Sam. A murder is bad enough, but this place was like a tinderbox even before this happened. This will make it ten times worse. I don't know if we can take it. I can't even count the number of fistfights I've broken up in the last six months. And death threats to me. I stopped counting," he said, then let out a long sigh.

"Do you know who has been making them?" I said.

"Not really. Some are not even from around here. I get them on the phone, in the mail, and over the fax. I even had one sent FedEx to me from Alaska. *FedEx!*"

"Are they all ranchers?" I said.

"People don't normally sign death threats, so I don't know for sure, but not all of them take a rancher's point of view. A lot of them are people who say I'm taking too long with my biological survey. Or I'm not following the law. A lot of the ones I get from outside of Red Creek are from environmentalists."

"Did you ever get one from Ty Jones?"

"I didn't even know Ty Jones before this happened, so I'm not sure if I did. But as far as I know, I didn't. Leland called me today and asked me the same question. I used to keep track of all of them but I stopped about six months ago. He came by about an hour ago and picked up what I had," he said.

"If I understand this right, before you can add a species to the Endangered Species List, the U.S. Fish and Wildlife Service must first complete some kind of study which either concludes that the species is in danger of extinction or not," I said.

"It's a little more complicated than that, but that is essentially it," he said after considering a much longer answer.

"And where are you in that process?" I said.

"Well, we are in the process of collecting the final sets of data. That should be done within the week. From that data, I will write a draft biological survey. Then there will be a public comment period."

"With what you have now, how does it look?"

"It's really impossible to say without having all the data,

but I have seen a few surprising things. We'll have to wait and see.''

''Like what?''

''I wouldn't mind giving the senator a little heads-up on the draft before I release it, but I would really prefer to finish looking at the data first,'' he said.

''Okay, that's fair. What happens after the public comment period?'' I asked.

''We make any appropriate changes and issue the final report,'' he said.

''After the report, what?''

''If the report comes back that the species is endangered, then it will be added to the list, and we begin making a management plan. That plan would be the instrument used to protect the endangered species, usually by protecting its habitat,'' he explained.

''And that is where the ranchers believe they'll lose out?''

''That's right. They think we will find that the same lakes and streams they use in the ranching operations are the critical habitat for the yellow-backed minnow. And to be honest, if that is the finding we will have to put some limits on the use of those lakes and streams.''

''Limits? What kind?'' I asked.

''That's impossible to say at this point. But it could be drastic, and then again the changes we have to make may cause them only minor inconveniences. Do you mind if we go outside? I need a smoke,'' he said.

''Oh no, not at all, but I'm done unless you have any questions for me.''

I drove back out to the airport, turned in my rental car, and tried to call Maggie from a pay phone. She was not at the office and did not answer her mobile phone.

Chapter Nine

As I boarded the plane, I asked the flight attendant if we would make it back to Wasatch City on schedule. She thought we would. Good, that would give me plenty of time to deplane and find Tracey and a TV to watch the six o'clock news.

The flight was uneventful and Tracey was waiting at the gate for me when the plane arrived. I knew it had been a hard day. They always are at this point in a campaign. But you could not tell it by looking at Tracey—her eyes were bright and her demeanor relaxed. She looked as if she was ready to put in another fourteen hours.

I briefed her on everything that had happened since we last spoke. She told me that Maggie had tracked down Vernon about one o'clock this afternoon and was worried about what he might have said to Hardcopy.

We found a little bar off the main concourse with a TV, ordered something to drink, and waited for the news. Unfortunately, we didn't have to wait long. It was the lead story on the six o'clock news:

67

Anchor: Good evening, everyone, and thanks for tun-
ing into Channel 7 News. Details of the investigation
into the murder of Steve Tate are beginning to leak
out of Red Creek tonight. Channel 7's own John Mayfield is in Red Creek. John, can you tell us what is
going on there tonight?

Hardcopy was standing in front of the Old Courthouse
wearing a denim shirt, blue jeans, and a pair of what looked
like brand-new cowboy boots. I was willing to bet he had
bought them just for this show.

"Well, Jean, the investigation here in Red Creek seems
to center on a man by the name of Tyson Jones, a twenty-
eight-year-old native of Gunlock, a small town about thirty
miles north of here. Jones was arrested last night at a local
bar. Sources close to the arrest say that he was so inebriated
at the time that sheriff's officials are still unable to question
him about the murder.

"But KFTV has learned that Jones has made repeated
threats against Tate in the past and has served time on a
conviction related to those threats. Six months ago Tate was
appearing on a Wasatch City radio station talking about
environmental issues when the threat was received. Earlier
today, KFK released that portion of the show."

The screen changed from Hardcopy to the animated picture of a reel-to-reel tape recorder and the following transcript:

Announcer: You are listening to KFK Radio, all news
all the time. We are in the studio with environmental
activist Steve Tate, and he is taking your calls.
Caller [presumed to be Jones]: Steve Tate, we know
where you live and you are going to die.

"That call was later traced to a bunkhouse on a ranch
owned by Vernon Hansen where Jones had been employed

by Hansen as a ranch hand. Vernon Hansen is the brother of U.S. senator Maggie Hansen and also Sheriff Leland Hansen of Creek County, who is heading up this investigation.''

A picture of all three appeared on the screen.

''Vernon Hansen sat down for a wide-ranging interview earlier this afternoon. I think you'll be surprised by what we learned.''

The shot changed again from a live shot to the video footage of Hardcopy and Vernon sitting at what looked like a kitchen table.

Vernon: I guess I've known Ty all my life. He's had his problems but he was a good boy. I believe that.

Hardcopy: Yet he's known to have threatened Steve Tate and is being held in jail for questioning in his murder.

Vernon: Well, it was never proved that Ty threatened Steve.

Hardcopy: Well, how would you explain the threatening calls made from your bunkhouse?

You could tell by the look on Vernon's face that he had not expected the reporter to know so much. He shifted in his seat and rubbed his face as though he were thinking about the question.

Vernon: I really never knew what to make of all that.

Hardcopy: He did have a bomb. He pled guilty to that.

Vernon: Yeah, but he told me he'd never even seen that thing until Leland showed it to him at the jail.

Hardcopy: So you think he was framed. Who would do such a thing to Ty?

Vernon: Now hold on a minute. I never said that. You're trying to—

Hardcopy: Then you don't believe Ty Jones—

Vernon: You don't know what we've been up against over here for the last five or six years with this yellow-backed minnow thing. It's only a slim fish that grows no longer than three inches. People are scared.

Hardcopy: Scared of what?

Vernon: It is our way of life being taken away from us. We've built something here in Red Creek. A heritage that was passed to us by our parents that we would like to pass to our children. And people like Steve Tate want to take that away. And they do it by trying to make people believe they are protecting something. That's a lie, pure and simple. What they're really doing is trying as hard as they can to destroy something. They don't care about the yellow-backed minnow. It's a tool, a means to an end. All they care about is ending ranching, and about making Red Creek a ghost town. That's all. The rest of it is just lies. I mean, look at what he was doing when he was killed—shooting cattle and destroying private property. They don't respect people's property rights. Stuff like that don't mean a thing to people like Steve.

Hardcopy: Stuff like what?

Vernon: Private property, private property rights. They want to control everything—their property, my property, and yours.

Hardcopy: Have you and Ty Jones ever talked about this?

Vernon: Oh, I don't know. Ranching is, or was, his livelihood. He knows what's at stake.

Hardcopy: How about your sister, Senator Hansen, and your brother the sheriff—do they share your feelings?

Vernon: Well, of course they do. They can't say it like I can because they're politicians. But in private they'll tell you. They know it's wrong.

The shot changed back to Hardcopy standing in front of the Old Courthouse.

Hardcopy: The line in the sand has been drawn pretty clearly here in Red Creek, and Steve Tate quite literally got caught in the crossfire. The only question now is will justice be served. Back to you, Jean.

I had a pit in my stomach big enough to fall into. I could not believe it. Even if you know they're coming, bad stories always seem worse when you see them on the screen or in print. My worst fears played out on statewide TV. Vernon had just confirmed every doubt about Maggie's environmental positions. All along her enemies, including Jeff Montgomery, had accused her of crass political maneuvering. Even though Maggie's opinions on environmental issues had become quite moderate, there was an element of truth to those accusations. Now her own brother had confirmed—on video—that their suspicions had been well founded. As in most cases in politics, the truth is of little relevance, because perception is reality. I could not imagine how the story could have been worse.

And from the look on Tracey's face, she couldn't either. We finished our drinks in silence, pretending to watch the rest of the newscast. Even though my eyes were on the TV, all I could think about was how to handle Vernon's latest sound bite.

"Not a lot of options on this one, are there?" Tracey said after she finished her drink.

"Nope. If it had been anybody but her brother we'd have some options. But her own brother. Normally you'd go after the person's credibility," I said.

"Yeah, and if we go too far in contradicting him the media will try to get us in a he-said-she-said."

"I can see it now. 'Mr. Hansen, your sister says you have no right misrepresenting her positions on environmental issues. How do you respond to that?' 'It all goes back to what I said the first time, Mr. Hardcopy. She can't say what's really on her mind because she is trying to get votes. So I have to say it for her,' '' I said.

Tracey forced the kind of laugh that masks anxiety.

"So how do we handle this one?" I said.

"First of all, we don't let Maggie talk to the media. Then I'll respond to all the media inquiries in person. We won't issue a press release or anything like that," she said.

"That's about the only thing we can do. And all you say is that Maggie stands by her record on environmental issues. That her opinions and positions are well known and have been debated in this state for years. Just refuse to comment on what he said, kind of a no comment without actually saying 'no comment.' They ask the questions they want answered. You answer the questions you want asked. You know what I mean?" I said.

"Oh yeah, do it all the time. Off the record, I can point out that Vernon opposed us on the Jacob Mountain Wilderness Area bill too. He was pretty tough on her then," she said.

"I had forgotten how vocal he was back then," I said.

"So no matter what they ask, I'll just restate our position," she said.

"And if they ask what Vernon meant when he said this or that just tell 'em they'll have to ask Vernon," I said.

"That's a little risky, don't you think?" she asked.

"Yeah, but not as risky as interpreting what he said and creating the possibility of him contradicting us," I said.

"Can't Maggie or Leland talk to him? Get him to tone it down?" she said.

"He's a loose cannon. The best thing we can do is stay out of his sights," I said.

"All right, what's next?" she said.

"Let's go back to the office and take whatever media

calls come in tonight. Then maybe we can grab some dinner later if you're hungry," I said.

"That sounds good," she said. "But I need to make a phone call before we leave."

"Did you already have plans?"

"Nothing important."

"Do you want me just to handle the media calls tonight? I don't mind."

"No, absolutely not. I want to do it," she said.

"Can you just move the plans until later? I'm sure we'll be done by nine. Don't you think?"

"Probably, but this is nothing important. It'll wait."

She made her call and I called Maggie. She had not seen the story. She was furious when I told her what Vernon had said.

"Listen, why don't you call Leland and tell him what happened. I'm sure he doesn't know either. Ask him how he thinks we ought to handle it and I'll call you when we get to the office," I said.

"I'll call Leland, but I'm going to call Vernon and give him a piece of my mind. He has got to stop this," she said.

"Maggie, you know your brother better than me, but I don't think that will work. Let's just call Leland first, think about it for a while, and then decide how to handle Vernon," I said.

"It never hurts to think about something like this," she said more to herself than me. Maggie often took my advice but not always. I was hoping she would this time.

"You're right," she continued. "But Sam, this is family and I am going to handle it."

I was not sure what she meant by that. I could tell by the tone of her voice that whatever she meant, it was not up for negotiation, so I just said, "Okay."

Tracey and I drove to the office and she caught me up on what had happened at campaign headquarters. When we got there Mike was still working in his office. He was glad

I was back because he had several questions about the projects he was working on. I took about an hour to go over things with him and made sure everything that needed to be done was getting done, and to Mike's credit that appeared to be the case. I was a little bit annoyed at myself for not having turned more of this stuff over to Mike before. He was doing a good job and it would have made my life a lot simpler.

As expected there were several calls about the Channel 7 News report, which Tracey handled just like we had planned. About nine o'clock, we dialed Maggie again and put her on the speakerphone.

"I called Leland like you suggested," she said. "He had seen the newscast already. There really wasn't much I could do. I guess he called Vernon and let him have it."

"How did Vernon take it?" Tracey said.

"Vernon's very shrewd when it comes to ranching and most other things, but when it comes to politics, he has a blind spot. He doesn't understand it. He's like my mother that way. The difference is my mother stayed away from reporters; Vernon is drawn to them by some overwhelming supernatural force.

"The good news is," she continued, "I don't think we will have to worry about distancing ourselves from what Vernon said. Leland will do it for us."

"What do you mean?" I said.

"Well, like we said earlier, we can't go after Vernon because it would make us look bad. But Leland's not up for election, and even if he were, this thing wouldn't hurt him."

"That's right," Tracey said.

"So tomorrow when the media calls to get an update on the case and asks him about Vernon's remarks, he'll just say that Vernon doesn't speak for him and has no business doing so," she said.

"Maggie, would he say that while he agrees with many

of Vernon's environmental positions? He knows that you don't always agree with him," I said.

"I don't think he'll say that, and I wouldn't ask him to. Plus, it puts him in the position of defending everything Vernon says. He's smart enough not to get himself in that position," Maggie said.

"Okay, okay. I just thought it would help put some distance between us and Vernon," I said.

"You mean between us and Vernon's comments, don't you?" Maggie said.

"Right." It wasn't really what I meant, but I knew Maggie was sending me a message. *"Be careful how you handle Vernon. He's family."* The Hansens are a close family; not even politics gets in the way of that.

"This is the way I want this handled," she said. "Leland has been doing this for years. It's how their relationship works and he can handle this for us."

"There is no question that Leland can handle it," I said.

"So we'll just keep restating your position on environmental issues, refuse to comment directly on Vernon's remarks, and rely on Leland to do the rest," Tracey said.

"That's right," Maggie said.

"I'm sure Montgomery will club us over the head with this one tomorrow night," I said.

"Yes, but he would have done that anyway," said Tracey.

"But this makes his attacks a hundred times more credible," I said. I was beginning to worry that Maggie would feel more compelled to defend Vernon than her record. That would be a disaster, but I knew the time was not right to talk about that, so I let it go.

"Listen, if I can't handle some pretty boy like Jeff Montgomery, I don't deserve to be in the United States Senate," Maggie said.

I have never known a candidate who was not overconfident about his or her debate skills. Fortunately Maggie was usually able to back up her bravado. But this one was going to be tricky.

After talking with Maggie I went to my office and sorted through a stack of phone messages several inches thick to see if there were any that could not wait until tomorrow. As usual, there were a few that needed immediate attention. So I took about ten minutes to return those while Tracey finished up her work for the day. When I had finished, I gathered up a few things I wanted to take home to read and went to Tracey's office. Mike was still in the office with a group of volunteers who had taken a break from stuffing mailers to have pizza.

Tracey was working on her computer when I walked in.

"Do you think you could get your other plans back on track? I hate to take you away from that," I said.

"No, it's no big deal. He knows what my job is like. He kind of expects it," she said, not looking up from her computer. She was obviously engrossed in what she was doing, so I sat quietly while she finished.

In about five or six minutes she turned off her computer and reached in her purse and retrieved some lipstick, a small mirror, and a compact. She touched up her makeup, threw a few things in her purse, and was ready to go.

We decided to go to one of the trendy new brew pubs that were opening all over Wasatch City. It was late enough that we were seated without a wait. I ordered a roasted chicken salad and she ordered a burger with fries. I wished that I could eat like that and remain as thin as she was.

Tracey and I had worked together for almost a year. I hired her in Washington, D.C., to be the senator's director of communications based on her reputation for being a good writer as well as having a savvy approach to media relations. And she had lived up to that billing. She didn't back away from the hard issues and wasn't timid in ad-

vocating difficult positions—even ones she did not neces-
sarily agree with.

But we did not really know each other outside of the
work relationship. She had always been professional in her
conduct in the office, and I have always tried to do the
same. And in the 90s that meant that there wasn't an abun-
dance of talk around the office about people's personal
lives. In fact this was probably the first time we had seen
each other in what could be described as a social setting,
and even then we spent most of the evening talking about
work. When our desserts arrived—I was having sorbet and
she was having chocolate cheesecake—she asked, "How
did you come to work for the senator?"

"It's kind of a boring story, but I like telling it if you're
sure you want to hear it," I said. Every once in a while, I
dust off my sense of modesty and give it a workout just in
case I ever need it.

"Sure," she said. "The night is young."

"During Maggie's first campaign I was in high school.
I was taking civics from one of these life-changing teach-
ers. You know the kind I'm talking about—they don't
teach as much as they help you learn. Know what I mean?"

She nodded.

"Well, he decided that we should all get some hands-on
experience at how political campaigns are run. So he con-
tacted both candidates for the U.S. Senate and told them
that his class would take responsibility for delivering pam-
phlets and things to the voting precincts around the high
school. Everybody in the class had to sign up to help one
of the candidates. I signed up for Maggie mainly because
there were more people on her list and I thought it would
be less work.

"But I missed the first meeting of my group and in my
absence I was elected team captain. Needless to say, I
haven't missed a meeting like that since. Anyway, I orga-
nized the whole thing and when Maggie came to speak at

our class I got to introduce her and escort her around the school.

"After a while, I ended up actually getting into it. I really kind of liked it. I had the maps up in my bedroom and I was helping people get their routes done. Everything. Of course, Maggie won, and I got a handwritten note from her in the mail about two weeks later. It said, 'I couldn't help but notice that I won in the precincts you helped me in. Thank you very much. Come see me in six years and I'll have you do all of them.' By that time, I was hooked.

"I volunteered on Congressional campaigns during the next two cycles. Six years later, I was a senior in college and Maggie was up for her first reelection. I called her campaign manager and made an appointment. It's kind of a long story but Maggie remembered me and I ended up getting hired as their grassroots coordinator. A full-time staff position. But since the job required mostly afternoon and evening hours, I was still able to finish my degree. My grades took a nosedive, but it was worth it."

"What did you major in?" she asked.

"Political science, what else?" I said. "How about you?"

"Communications and journalism," she said. "So what happened after the campaign?"

"Maggie came into my office the day after the election and said, 'Since we probably destroyed your grade point average, the least we could do is offer you a job in Washington.'

"I was ecstatic over the opportunity. And I loved the job. I really liked Maggie. During the next two election cycles, I would take a leave of absence and come back here and work on the campaigns, so by the time Maggie's next reelection rolled around I was by far the most qualified person to run the campaign, which had been my plan all along. She hired me and I ran it.

"By that time I was becoming a threat or at least a perceived threat to Maggie's chief of staff. We fought back and forth as to who was really in charge during the whole campaign. When the campaign was over, she walked into Maggie's office and said, 'Senator, you are going to have to choose between me and Sam.' I'm sure she thought Maggie would choose her.

"Maggie asked if she was sure she wanted to do this.

" 'I don't think it would be the best thing for anybody for both of us to keep working together here. I can't fire him, so you have to decide,' " she said.

" 'Well, if you are going to make me choose, I'll have to choose Sam,' " Maggie said. " 'I'll accept your resignation whenever you're ready, but just remember it doesn't have to be this way.' "

"It was obvious that she had overplayed her hand and the only way to save face was to resign. And she did. The next day, Maggie gave me the job."

"What a stupid thing to do. I mean the old chief of staff. You know, forcing Maggie's hand. I can't believe I said that," Tracey's face was bright red.

I started to laugh. I had never seen her flustered like that before.

"Don't worry. I'm usually the one with a foot in his mouth."

"I can't believe I said that like that. I obviously didn't mean that the way it came out. But that was a stupid move on the old chief of staff's part. Don't you think?" she said, trying to recover.

"I've always liked to think so," I said. "How about you? How did you get started in this business?"

"In college, I guess. I was at the University of Maine in communications and I took an internship in Washington. I interned in this freshman congressman's office with his press secretary. The congressman was not all that smart and had a habit of saying a lot of stupid things. Like he would constantly misstate his positions—saying he was going to vote against something that he planned to vote for. Oh, and he would often contradict himself in the same press conference. So it was kind of baptism by fire, but I liked it.

"After I graduated I took a job at a newspaper, but I didn't really like it. I had always wanted to be a reporter, but my experience in Washington had taught me that I really liked being an advocate.

"I hung on at the paper for about a year, then I called some of my friends in Washington to help me find a job there. But you know how Washington is. You've got to be there to get a job. So I ended up quitting the paper and moving to Washington. My parents thought I was crazy. My whole life I had wanted to be a reporter; now I had the job and I was quitting it to look for something else.

"They have to be pretty happy with the way things have turned out," I said.

"Oh yeah. It took me about three months to find a job. But once I did, they could see a career track in front of me and they calmed down a little bit. Now if I would just get married, their life's mission would be complete," she said.

"Are you an only child?" I asked.

"No, just the last to get married," she said.

"I guess the pressure is really on, then," I said.

"You don't want to know," she said, and then winked at me—or was it just a blink? I couldn't tell.

Suddenly I realized I was staring at her trying to decide if it had been a wink or a blink. Now it was my turn to be embarrassed.

"Any prospects out there?" I said as nonchalantly as I could.

"I've gotten my parents' hopes up a few times, but things never seemed to work out for one reason or another," she said. I suddenly realized that I was intensely curious about her current interest and hoped she would fill me in. But she didn't.

After that, I carefully charted the conversation back into

safer territory. We finished our desserts and she dropped me off at my apartment.

The maid service had been by the day before and I could see my floor again. I bagged my dirty laundry and left it by the door so I wouldn't forget to take it with me in the morning and went to bed. That night was one of those rare nights that even though I had a million and one things to worry about, I was too tired to worry and slept without dreams until the alarm went off at 5:30 A.M.

My brief years in politics have added at least one quirk to my personality—I can never really relax in the morning until I see what's in the *Capitol Times*. I fished some gym shorts out of my dirty laundry bag, donned a pair of jogging shoes and a T-shirt, and decided to go for my monthly jog. There is a great little coffeehouse about a mile and a half from my apartment with a newsstand right next door. About once a month, I jog over (I normally dress for jogging but walk), take about thirty minutes to catch my breath, order a cup of coffee and a scone, and read the *Capitol Times, New York Times*, and the *Washington Post*.

After I had jogged over and bought the papers, I scanned the *Capitol Times* while I stood in line to order coffee. There was a follow-up story on the murder, updating the investigation. But just as I had suspected, at the bottom of the story was an editor's note: *Wayne Smith assisted in compiling this story.* Smitty was gradually taking over this story; the next one would be under Smitty's byline and the gloves would be off. I ordered my coffee and scone, took a small table by the window, and read the story. There wasn't anything new in the story until I got to the portion of the story I could tell Smitty had written.

. . . the cattle being destroyed by Tate, at the time he was murdered, were owned by a rancher named Vernon Hansen [a file photograph of Vernon accompanied the story]. Vernon is the brother of Creek County sheriff Leland Hansen and Utah's Senior United States senator Maggie Hansen.

Vernon Hansen has become an increasingly important part of this case. He is also the former employer of Ty Jones, who is being held in the Creek County jail for questioning regarding the murder. [Ty's story was explained in detail earlier in the story.]

In addition, the *Capitol Times* has learned that as in the previous case, Vernon Hansen retained and paid for an attorney to represent Mr. Jones.

"Ty comes from a good family. I've known his mother for thirty years or more. I don't abandon people in their time of need," said Hansen.

The sheriff's office is also working on another lead. It seems that before his death Mr. Tate had been involved with Sharon Watts, daughter of Wilson Watts, founder and chairman of the board of Watts World Wide, an international paper and textile concern.

Sharon Watts is expected to return to Red Creek in the near future to answer questions about the murder and her simultaneous departure from Red Creek. Sources close to the investigation believe Watts will eventually be cleared of any wrongdoing in the murder.

This was like the Chinese water drip torture. Every time I thought I had my arms around this situation, some new little facts dripped out. How did Smitty find this stuff out? I wondered who the "sources close to the investigation" were. Smitty must have a network of informants that would rival the CIA. I was willing to bet that even Leland didn't know that Vernon was paying for Ty's lawyer. If he had, I was sure he would have mentioned it.

I did not like the way this story was shaping up. I knew that this was going to be bad, but I had no idea how tightly

Vernon was going to bind Maggie to this story. Now, not only did we have a political problem, but Maggie's family was being tied closer and closer to the murder itself.

This was not a good trend.

Chapter Ten

I jogged as far as I could and walked the rest of the way back to the apartment. I called Tracey to make sure she had seen the story. She had. She also pointed out to me a little blurb in the "Tomorrow" section on the front page, which is a list of stories the paper is working on for tomorrow's paper.

It said, *Tomorrow the Capitol Times will begin a three-part series on the environmental struggles in Red Creek.*

We decided there really wasn't much we could do about Vernon paying for Ty's lawyer, and I was willing to bet that Maggie wasn't willing to do anything about it either. Tracey thought that from our perspective reporters would only be interesting in knowing if Maggie knew Ty Jones and if she knew her brother was paying his legal bills. Fortunately, we could answer no to both of those questions.

I showered, dressed, and went to Maggie's. She lived on the east side of Wasatch City in an area known as College

Grove. Maggie's husband was a named partner in a down-town law firm, and they enjoyed a pretty good lifestyle. (If you don't consider that Maggie spent about 180 days a year on the East Coast and another twenty-five days a year traveling to other parts of the country and world.)

Their lawn was immaculately groomed and the house spotless. It's the kind of house I don't feel comfortable in. Everything looked expensive and well kept. It just didn't feel lived in. Maggie answered the door while putting in her last earring.

"I'm glad you're here," she said. "I guess you've seen the paper."

"Oh yes. I assume you didn't know that Vernon was paying Ty's attorney."

"No. No, I didn't. I called Leland and he didn't know either. I guess he assumed the boy's mother was paying for it."

"Has anybody talked to Vernon?" I said.

"No, I was about to call him when you arrived. I'll call him now though."

We walked to her study. It was the only house I'd ever seen with his-and-her studies. She called Vernon, but there was no answer at his house or his office.

"Leland said that he would probably see him this morning. I asked him to call me after he talks to him," she said.

There was a knock on the door and Maggie said, "Would you get that? I'm sure it's Tracey." It was. I escorted her back to Maggie's study where we started going over the issues that would likely come up in the debate.

We worked in Maggie's study until about lunchtime. I went to the kitchen to grab some drinks while Tracey and Maggie worked on the opening and closing statements. I used Maggie's phone to order some lunch from a takeout Chinese place near the university and then called Leland to check on the investigation. His receptionist patched me through to his mobile phone.

"I'm on my way back to the office to meet with Sharon Watts," he said.

"When did she get to Red Creek?"

"Her lawyers called me this morning and said they were flying in at eleven-thirty and wondered if I could meet with them then. So that's where I'm headed."

"I thought there weren't any eleven-thirty flights into Red Creek," I said.

"There ain't unless your daddy owns his own jet. Watch the noon news on Channel 7; I bet they'll have it on there. Hardcopy asked me about the girl after reading the *Capitol Times* this morning, so he knows she's flying in on a private jet. I'm sure he'll be out there with a camera."

"He won't be able to stay away from that one," I said. I looked at my watch; it was five minutes to noon.

"Leland, who is this 'source close to the investigation' Smitty quoted this morning?" I asked.

"Danged if I know. You got any ideas?" he said. There was a barely perceptible accusatory tone in his voice.

"No, but it makes me nervous. That little leak didn't hurt us too much, but the next one might," I said.

"I brought my people together this morning and came down on them pretty hard about this kind of stuff. I hope it works. I suggest you do the same up there," he said. I made a mental note to be on the lookout for whoever it was.

Leland and I finished our conversation. Other than this Watts girl coming into Red Creek, nothing new had developed.

Maggie had a small TV in her kitchen, which I tuned to Channel 7 so I could watch the news for a while. Sure enough right at the top of the newscast was Hardcopy still in his brand-new cowboy boots. I was sure they were new now because he was limping as if he were suffering from the kind of blisters you get when you are breaking in a new pair of boots.

"Sources close to the investigation confirm that Ms. Watts is returning to Red Creek to face questions in connection with the murder of Steve Tate," Hardcopy said. I had to laugh; his "sources close to the investigation" was Smitty.

On the picture was a video of the plane landing; it was a Gulf IV Lear jet with the company logo for Watts World Wide painted on the side. Next was a shot of Sharon Watts and what looked like her father and her attorneys getting off the plane. I would have bet anything that that was the first time an Armani suit had been in Red Creek.

"We'll continue following this developing story and have a live update tonight during the six o'clock news," Hardcopy said.

I poured the drinks and went back to Maggie's study where she and Tracey were still at work. I told them about the Sharon Watts entourage arriving in Red Creek.

We worked the debate preparation for several more hours, stopping only to eat the takeout when it arrived. After lunch I talked to Maggie about not getting bogged down in defending Vernon's recent statement but to simply state a positive position and point to things in her record that supported that. She gave me a sharp look that said, "I'll handle this the way I want to."

We touched on a couple of more issues and left so Maggie could get some rest.

Tracey and I went back to the office. I now had almost two days of messages that needed to be returned. But the first call I had to make was to Leland. He had been meeting with Sharon Watts for four hours and I wondered how it was going. I called his office and got his secretary.

"Oh, is this Sam? Okay yes, the sheriff asked me to interrupt him if you call. Hang on. Can you?" she said.

"Yes, thank you," I said and started sorting through my messages, sorting them by order of importance so that at least I would get to the important ones before I had to leave for the debate.

"Sam, how you doing? Sorry to make you wait," Leland said.

"Oh, no problem. How did it go with the Wattses?" I said.

"Pretty good; I guess it's just what I suspected," he said. "I don't know if you saw it on TV or not but she flew in with her army of lawyers. Ray and I met with them for about three hours this afternoon."

"What did you find out?" I said.

"If everything checks out, she's clean," he said.

It's hard to know how you're supposed to feel in those situations, but to be honest I was a little disappointed that it appeared she had not done it.

"What's her story? Can you tell me?" I said.

"Appears she's got an airtight alibi, starting Saturday morning at 11:10 when she flew out of here. You know how they check your ID when you fly now. And she got all her boarding passes. They got an army of PIs interviewing the crew and passengers on both flights she was on to Denver. Once she landed in Denver, her mother picked her up and has been with her ever since, even slept in the same room."

"PI?" I asked.

"Private investigators," he said.

"Oh," I said, feeling pretty stupid.

"Anyways, they sent a pretty clear message. The lead lawyer got mad and started pointing his finger at my chest, saying that they were all over this thing and if I made one wrong move it would take ten years to dig out from under all the lawsuits they'd file. Her dad was fuming about Smitty's story. Sometimes these 'sources close to the investigation' think they're helping you out, but they're really making things a lot more difficult,'' he said.

''Anyways they made it pretty clear that they'll do anything to prove she's innocent, and fortunately I think she is. 'Cause I'd hate to go toe-to-toe with those people. But I sent them a pretty clear message too. I'm running this investigation and I intend to track down every lead until I find the murderer.

''By the time they left, I think we understood each other,'' he said. ''They're probably hiring more lawyers right now.''

I wrapped up the call with Leland, and finished returning my calls and held a staff meeting just to make sure everything was going as smoothly as it appeared. Luckily it was; Mike was doing a good job. Tracey, Mike, and I had a meeting to discuss what we would do in the event of some kind of a meltdown during the debate tonight. Tracey would accompany Maggie to the debate and would handle the press there. Mike and I would watch from the campaign office in case some type of statement needed to be sent out. We planned to meet back here after the debate.

I hate debates. Nothing good can happen at a debate. Yet there is this perception that the stakes are so high and therefore every mistake is magnified a hundred times by the media. But in reality rarely, if ever, do debates affect the outcome of a race. You have to go as far back as 1960 to find any agreement on when the last presidential debate affected the outcome of the race. And in that particular case there were three extenuating circumstances. First, it was the first televised debate ever in the history of presidential politics. Second, it was a real debate where there was a free exchange of ideas between the candidates instead of the staged exchanges of canned sound bites we see now. Third, it was a close race. It was decided by less than one vote per precinct. And when the margins are that thin, there are hundreds if not thousands of things you can point to that made a difference, and in the Kennedy/Nixon campaign the debate was one of them. Sure, there have been other bad debate performances, but none that affected the outcome of an election.

But our debate had an interesting angle—the Tate murder. We were at a pivotal moment in the maturation of the story. Tomorrow the *Capitol Times* would begin a three-part series on Red Creek and when that was finished the maturation would be complete. But if Montgomery were smart, he could use this debate as a forum for defining the issues surrounding the murder.

I knew the Montgomery campaign was wrestling with what they should do. There is an axiom in politics: if your opponent is shooting himself in the foot, don't interrupt. I was certain that they could see this story turning against us. And that was what they needed. Some stories have to be helped along by the campaign press secretary actively going out and selling the story to the media. Other stories sprout legs without any help from the campaign, but even in this case the stories need to be framed by a campaign to have the greatest impact. I knew the Montgomery people were trying to decide what kind of story this was going to be.

Where I saw the story's potential to linger to the end of the campaign and swing the election in Montgomery's favor, they saw as a chance to get off the defensive for the first time during this election. If I had been running the Montgomery campaign, I would not have the self-control to let the story develop along its natural course. I would use this debate to frame the issue and use it as a launching pad to begin an unrelenting attack on Maggie's environmental positions.

There was a potential downside for Montgomery if he overplayed his hand. The one thing he had to avoid was a backlash against him for trying to capitalize on a murder.

But if he did it right, that damage would be minimal and it could completely change the dynamic of the race, giving Montgomery a real chance to win. And Montgomery was exactly the kind of politician who could carry this attack.

The debate was at 6:30 P.M. Mike and I were in my office watching a small television set I kept on my bookshelf for just such occasions.

The debate began with an introduction of both candidates. Jeff Montgomery was in his late thirties and a lawyer with a prestigious downtown law firm. He had made a name for himself as the U.S. attorney for Utah, where he had uncovered and prosecuted a massive price-fixing scheme among primary-care hospitals in the state.

There were two schools of thought of Montgomery. One said that he was nothing more than a blow dryer and a nice suit. That even though the case against the healthcare providers was complicated, he took all the credit while others did the brainwork. Others believed that yes, he was nice-looking and very media savvy, but there was also some intellectual weight there. He was the lead prosecutor in the case and those that watched him in action said that he handled the examination and cross-examinations of witnesses with little input from the other attorneys at his table. Thinking on his feet, never hesitating to go in for the kill when he could sense the time was right, backing off when the facts were not in his favor.

I had watched him now for almost fourteen months of this campaign and was convinced that the latter was true. He was polished and given to speaking in sound bites, but underneath that veneer was a sophisticated, complex man and a very capable politician. In essence, it was the worst of all possible scenarios for Maggie. If he beat her in this debate, it would prove that Maggie was losing her edge—unable to hold her own against a lightweight like Montgomery. If she won, it proved nothing—Montgomery was clearly out of her league to begin with.

The first thirty minutes of the debate were dedicated to foreign affairs. When we were negotiating to have the debate format I had insisted that it be first, because no one really cares about that stuff and hopefully the few people that would ordinarily watch something like this would turn it off out of sheer boredom. Even I could barely keep my own eyes open through the discussion of third-world policy and NATO expansion. Mike had left my office twice, once to get a Diet Coke, once to use the bathroom.

After the first thirty-minute block, the station broke away for some commercials. When they came back the format turned to domestic policy. They started off with Taxes and the Budget. Politicians can always find some things to argue about there. There was about fifteen minutes left to go when the question of environmental policy came up. I could feel my entire stomach tighten into a knot no bigger than a marble as Montgomery started boring in.

He said:

I have always had a profound respect for nature and the unsurpassed beauty of the land we live in; its wonder and beauty cannot be equaled by man's accomplishments. Once we destroy a piece of our natural birthright, it is gone for good. My concern over the environment is one of the main reasons I got into the race for the United States Senate. I have two small children and I want to pass on to them something more than strip malls and condos. Here in Utah we have been given more than our share of nature's wonders. We have to respect that and own up to the responsibility we have as stewards of those wonders.

My concern is that we haven't lived up to that responsibility. Senator Hansen has paid lip service to the objectives of protecting our environment, but it has been a long string of hollow promises cynically designed to protect votes, not the environment. Even her own brother admits that she panders to our environmental concerns without really believing her own words.

If I am elected to the United States Senate you will see a new kind of leadership. I will not participate in the kind of demagoguery that creates the kind of atmosphere where people would rather resort to violence than abide by the law. I will find the right kind of balance that will protect as many valid interests as possible, but I will never sell out my children's—our children's—natural heritage and I will never give aid and comfort to those who would take the law into their own hands rather than submit to the will of the people.

And regardless of the outcome of this election I call on my opponent to make the same commitment. We need leadership, not reckless demagoguery and shameless vote pandering.

He had framed this issue about as well as it could be framed. And laid as much of the blame that he could for Tate's murder at Maggie's feet without creating a substantial backlash against himself. He had worked hard to prepare Maggie for this attack. She took a deep breath and responded.

For the last several years, we have been grappling with some very complex issues in the rural parts of this state, especially in my hometown of Red Creek. As your representative in the U.S. Senate I have dealt with these issues in the most straightforward way I can. Have I been right on every stand I've taken? Maybe not. But in most cases the wisdom of the path we have taken has been borne out in the end. And until this latest tragedy it appeared that we were moving toward a resolution of these problems, at least in Red Creek. What has happened there is a tragedy, and

I regret that it is even a part of this debate tonight. But I will never be part of politicizing a tragedy of this importance for political gain. Never. I won't do it. This job does not mean that much to me.

As for demagoguery, I'll leave it to the voters to decide who has resorted to demagoguery.

That was as good a recovery as I could have hoped for, but it didn't keep Montgomery from accomplishing his goal of framing the issue in his favor. He had also completed the process of politicizing the issue. That exchange would be the lead in all the stories about the debate. I knew that Smitty was already working on his. In my mind's eye I could picture him sitting at his computer terminal pounding away and I felt an overwhelming desire to slap that silly grin off his face.

There were a few more questions that went pretty much as scripted. Montgomery attacked Maggie's record at every chance, like any underdog should do. And Maggie ignored his attacks in favor of presenting a more positive agenda, like any good front runner should do.

When the debate was over I called Tracey on her mobile. She agreed with me that Montgomery had to be happy with how the debate went.

"The thing is," she said, "Maggie was in a no-win situation. Even if she'd hit a home run, which it just about was, it still wouldn't keep him from torquing up the pressure on us."

"That's true. How is she?" I said.

"I don't know, she's still on stage shaking hands and talking. I need to get out there," she said.

"Call me when you two are alone," I said.

"Okay," she said, and hung up.

After I hung up with Tracey, Mike said to me, "I wonder how all that played on C-SPAN?"

"On what?" I said.

"C-SPAN. You know."

"The debate?" I think I must have raised my voice, because Mike got this startled look on his face.

"They called today and said they were going to cover it live. I left you and Tracey a memo with the details," he said. I took a little pride in the fact that he was smart enough to leave a paper trail.

"Mike, that's not something you 'leave a memo' about. You've got to tell me stuff like that."

"Nobody watches C-SPAN," he said.

"Nobody in Utah watches C-SPAN. But the national media will, I mean, were watching. And if they missed it live, they'll catch it on one of the two million replays," I said.

"I didn't ask them to cover it. They did that all on their own," he said.

"I know, I know, it's just that it's a pretty big deal, that's all. I know it's not your fault. Don't worry," I said.

I looked at my watch. It was 9:30 P.M. on the East Coast. We would start getting calls tonight. Then I had another thought. If I were working this story from the Montgomery side, I would be sending clips of Smitty's story and a transcript of Vernon's interview with Hardcopy to every reporter with a fax machine.

I called a friend of mine at one of the East Coast newspapers and sure enough, they had received a fax with the story and the transcript about 3:30 local time today with a note to watch the debate on C-SPAN tonight. Montgomery's people were good.

Just then my phone rang.

"Answer that, Mike. If it's anyone but Tracey or Maggie take a message."

"Hansen for Senate, this is Mike."

Pause.

"Yeah, he's right here. Hang on." He handed the receiver to me and said, "It's Tracey."

"Tracey, did you know this thing was on C-SPAN?"

"The debate?" she said.

"Yep. And the Montgomery campaign sent out a media alert with the *Capitol Times* stories and a transcript of Hardcopy's interview with Vernon."

"How'd Montgomery know it was going to be on C-SPAN?" she said.

"They informed them about the same time they informed us, I imagine," I said. Mike looked down at his feet.

"No one informed me?" She made her statement into a question.

"Word didn't get to me either, but there's no use worrying about that now. Are you guys on your way over here?" I said.

"Just pulling into the parking garage," she said.

"See you in thirty seconds."

Minutes later we were all meeting in Maggie's office.

"This will be too tempting for the national media," Maggie said. "They're going to be all over this one."

"She's right," Tracey said, looking over at me. Everybody seemed to be waiting on me to pull a rabbit out of my hat and tell them how we were going to fix this one.

"There aren't any magic tricks here," I said. "There's been a murder; the senator's brother is connected with the leading suspect in that murder, the same brother who also has a motive to want Tate murdered, the same brother with no good alibi for the time of the murder; the murder is being investigated by the senator's other brother, and the victim was a prominent environmentalist. As far as I can see there is no way to spin ourselves out of this one. We'll just have to slog through it. It's our own personal Vietnam. We'll have to do our best and hope the good guys win this time," I said.

"Tracey and Mike, would you excuse us, please?" Maggie said while staring at me.

There was an awkward moment while Tracey and Mike got up and left the room, trying not to make eye contact with either Maggie or me. Mike was the last out and he shut the door.

"Okay, Sam, I want you to lay it all out right now. You think Vernon was involved in this murder somehow. Don't you?" she asked.

"The guy is a hothead, Maggie. Just look at what he's said and done since the murder."

"That's your opinion. And I guess I can't keep you from it. But I can tell you that I know Vernon much, much better than you and he would not do this. And I want you to keep your opinions about my brother to yourself," she said.

"I haven't told anybody about my opinions," I said.

"What do you call what just happened in here two minutes ago?" she said.

"Maggie, that is our situation, that is how the reporters are going to see this thing. That's how the stories are going to be written," I said.

"That's not true; they can't link Vernon to this thing that way," she said.

"Think about it, Maggie. It's all there right in front of them, they don't even have to dig for it," I said.

There was a long silence as Maggie thought over what I had said. She had dealt with the national and local media long enough to realize that I was right. I could see by the gradual change in the expression on her face that she agreed.

"Listen, that's the bad news," I said. "The good news is the forensic evidence that Leland is waiting on could clear Vernon. Or something else could break. From what I could tell, Leland is spending all his time on this thing. I'm sure he's convinced of Vernon's innocence too," I said.

"But you're right, that won't stop them from writing the story you just outlined," she said.

"No. No, it won't."

Chapter Eleven

Maggie, Tracey, and I spent the next minutes discussing how to handle the national media exposure. There really weren't any good answers; all we could do was answer their questions honestly and hope Leland arrested the murderer and that Vernon wasn't involved.

After our meeting, I was at my desk typing a to-do list for Mike when Maggie came in.

"I'm worried, Sam. You were right, it just doesn't look good," she said.

"I think everything will work out," I said.

"Maybe it will or maybe it won't. When I decided to run again, I knew I might lose. Of course any election can be lost, but last time I never really seriously entertained the idea. But this time it was different; I realized there were some very real vulnerabilities. But in the end, I decided I would rather lose than pass up the opportunity I had to accomplish some of the things I've been working on the last ten years. You know what I mean?"

I nodded, sensing that she had more to say.

"But I don't want to lose like this. This isn't right. If I were to lose on the issues, I could live with that. Out with the old, in with the new, that sort of thing. It would hurt, but I could live with it. But to go out on a scandal, you can never really fully recover your reputation. That's unacceptable to me."

"I'll do my best, Maggie. And right now things look a little on the bleak side. But who knows what tomorrow will bring."

"That's right, but nothing that is going to happen here in Wasatch City is going to affect the outcome of this race more than that murder investigation. Don't you agree?"

"I do."

"Well, I would feel better about this situation if I knew you were down there keeping an eye on it for me. Leland's got to run the investigation; he can't always be thinking about how it will affect me. And if you're not down there we'll find out everything about the time the media does. You know, sometimes a ten-minute heads-up is all you need. Don't you think?"

"I'll be on the ten-thirty flight."

Nina was gone, so I made my own plane reservation. I knew I would not be able to pick up a car until the next day; all the rental places would be closed when I arrived. I wondered how the idea of Maggie sending me down to watch things would sit with Leland. If I were him I would probably be offended. But Leland is a more secure person than I am and I guessed that he would be all right with it. I decided to give him a call just to smooth the way.

He had seen the debate and I told him about the situation with the national media.

"Maggie is nervous about what's going to happen next and she wants me to come down there so I can hear about things firsthand without having to bother you every ten minutes.''

''Good, we can have breakfast at the Creek Side every morning,'' he said.

''Sounds good to me,'' I said. All in the line of duty, of course.

'' 'Course, I don't mind you calling either,'' he said.

''Well, if it's just the same to you, I think Maggie would feel more comfortable if I were down there,'' I said.

''Good. Good. But don't get a hotel room. I got a house just off Jackson Street I usually rent out but I'm in between renters and you can stay there. You need a ride in from the airport?'' he said.

''That was my next question. If it's not too much trouble,'' I said.

''You on the ten-thirty flight?'' he asked.

''Yeah, gets in at eleven-fifty-five.''

''I'll meet you out front about midnight.''

''You're sure that's not too much trouble?''

''Oh, heavens no. I'll see you then.''

I asked Tracey to run me out to the airport again, even though it would have been more convenient to just drive myself and leave my car in long-term parking. I was really coming to respect Tracey's political judgment and wanted to go over everything with her one more time.

It was still only nine o'clock when we got to the airport so we decided to go in and grab a sandwich. We found a fast food restaurant on the main concourse and bought a couple of hamburgers and walked down to my gate.

''Do you do much hiking?'' she asked.

''Not as much as I like, but I love to go, especially around here. There are some great trails,'' I said.

''Where do you suggest? I thought I'd try to go this weekend.''

''Some of the best trails for this time of year are down

in Red Rock country around Red Creek. You should come down,'' I said. ''Or do you already have plans up here?''

''Actually, I did have plans, but they canceled. Can you believe it? This time *he* had to go out of town,'' she said.

''Well, you ought to come down. There's some great trails and it'll give you a chance to meet Leland.''

''I should probably stay around here, don't you think?''

Yes, I thought. ''No, it will be okay,'' I said. ''With a laptop and a phone line no one will know you're not here. Just come down after work tomorrow, we'll go hiking on Saturday, and you're back at the office on Sunday.''

''Sounds good.''

We finished our sandwiches and the announcer called my flight. On the flight down I thought about what I had just done. Any way you looked at it I had just made a date with a person over whom I had a supervisory role. When I made the date I wasn't really thinking of it as a date or I wouldn't have done it. I was thinking of it as more of a platonic thing. Two friends and coworkers going hiking together. Nothing wrong with that. But how was that different from a date in this case? If there were more than the two of us from the campaign then yes, it would be a legitimate work outing.

But Tracey didn't really see me as a coworker. The other night on the phone she had referred to me as her boss, which I was. Maybe she didn't really want to go but felt like she had to because I asked her to. She hadn't really jumped at the chance. I decided I'd better call her in the morning and back out. She would probably be relieved.

The plane arrived in Red Creek without incident and just as planned Leland was waiting for me out front.

''How was the flight?'' he asked.

''Uneventful,'' I said.

''That's the best kind,'' he said. ''I forgot to tell you when you called. The state crime lab called, said they finished the tests of the bullet and the tire tracks. They sent them FedEx for eight o'clock delivery tomorrow morning.''

''Did they tell you anything over the phone?'' I said.

''No, it was just some clerk that called; he hadn't even read the reports. Let's meet at the Creek Side at six-forty-five so we can be at the office at eight.''

''Sounds good,'' I said. I packed my jogging clothes this time.

The next morning I followed my usual morning ritual of finding and reading the *Capitol Times* before doing anything else. There were two stories on the front page, both of them written by Smitty, who was in his element now. One story was on the debate. The headline read MONT-GOMERY LASHES OUT AT HANSEN'S ENVIRONMENTAL REC-ORD, subhead: *Montgomery Calls on Hansen to Tone Down Excessive Rhetoric.*

It was a bad headline, and there wasn't much in the story that I didn't expect. It read in part:

... During the course of the debate, Montgomery launched a stinging, if inconsistent, attack on Hansen's environmental stands. On one hand he accused the senator of helping create the tension that many believe led to the murder of prominent environmentalist Steve Tate, but he also accused her of pandering to environmental voters by making hollow promises she never intended to keep.

For her part Hansen maintained the composure of a front runner and referred repeatedly to her record as one of balancing environmental concerns with economic reality. ...

The second headline was just as bad. It read: AN ENVI-RONMENT FOR MURDER, subhead:*The first in a three-part*

*series looking into the environmental movement in Red
Creek.*

The story told about the beginning of the environmental
movement in Red Creek, back when Omar Blackford was
the only one who cared. Unfortunately it also had a few
quotes from Maggie during that era. In the context of when
they were delivered I am sure they were fine, but read by
today's standards they sounded really reactionary. Back in
those days "environmentalist" was a pejorative, and that
is the way Maggie used it. Although I'm sure if you ex-
amined what other politicians at the time were saying it
would seem more moderate. But the *Capitol Times* was not
giving her the benefit. This was the kind of thing Montgomery had hoped for. One story calling on her to tone
down her rhetoric, another story reviving her oldest and
worst quotes. Both stories were well written and left us
with very little room to maneuver. Of course, we needed
to deny that we were or had been demagoguing this issue,
but with proof to the contrary being printed in the newspapers, even that was a delicate matter.

I finished reading the papers and met Leland at the Creek
side, where I indulged myself for the second time in three
days. When we finished eating we headed over to his office.
The test results from the state crime lab were not in yet so
I decided to return a few phone calls and check in with the
office. I called Tracey to cancel our plans for Saturday, but
she was not in. I had been returning phone calls and checking my voice mail for about thirty minutes when Leland
stuck his head into my office.

"I got the stuff. Ray's on his way over. Come on in,"
he said.

By the time I got off of the call I was on and walked
into Leland's office, Ray was already there. The report con-
sisted of ten or twelve typed pages and a few charts and
diagrams. Leland had three copies of the report made so
that we each would have a copy.

I read through mine, but did not understand a lot of what I read. I finished first and put my copy on Leland's desk and waited for him and Ray to finish and tell me what it all meant. It took them a while to finish as they kept referring back to previous parts of the reports and spent a lot of time going over the charts and graphs.

"What does all that tell us?" I asked when they had finished.

"Essentially we know what kind of tires left the tracks at the murder scene, and that it was a .22-caliber rifle that killed Tate," Leland said, leaning back in his chair and propping one foot on an open desk drawer.

"So you'll be able to tell if it was Ty's truck?" I asked.

"We'll be able to tell if his truck has the same kind of tires," said Ray.

"But this truck has two different kinds of tires on it. One kind on the front and one kind on the back. So it should be pretty easy to ID," said Leland.

"So it definitely was a truck?" I said.

"Yeah, both kinds of tires are truck tires. But it could be like a Ford Explorer or something like that," said Ray.

Leland picked up the phone and dialed it. "I'll have 'em check Jones's right now," he said as we waited for the phone to be answered.

"Yeah, this is Sheriff Hansen. I need somebody to go out to Ty Jones's truck and tell me the make of all four tires."

Pause.

"That's right. All four of 'em. I'll hold.

"We had the thing impounded when we arrested him," he said to Ray and me. We sat in silence as we waited on whoever was checking Ty's truck.

"Yeah, I'm here, go ahead," Leland finally said.

Pause.

"You're sure?" he said.

Pause.

"All right. Thank you," he said, and hung up.

"If Ty Jones did it he used somebody else's truck. His tires don't match. They're a different make and they are all four the same," he said.

"That would have been too easy," Ray said. "Now we got to send somebody out to check all the tires of the other ranchers who have leases up that canyon."

"I'll get somebody started on that as soon we get done here," said Leland.

"Make sure they look at all the trucks they have, not just the ones they drive personally," said Ray.

"Right, that's a good idea," said Leland.

"What about the bullet?" I asked.

"It was from a .22, fired from about fifteen feet. Killed. Instantly," Leland said.

"Lucky really, if you want to call it that. Unlucky for Steve, I guess. At that distance a .22-caliber is just as likely as not to ricochet off the skull as penetrate it. Could've just injured him," Ray said.

"That leads me in one of two directions," Leland said. "Either the killer had a lot of confidence in his marksmanship or it wasn't premeditated; he just found 'em up there shooting cattle and the .22 was all he had."

"Or he was like me and did not know anything about guns," I said.

"That's possible too, but I think one of Leland's scenarios is probably right," said Ray. "I'll bet ya one of these ranchers just found him up there, got mad, decided to go kill him, and all they had was a .22. So they used what they had."

"But if you shoot a man with a .22," I said, "given what you just said about ricocheting, wouldn't you at least walk over and make sure he was dead?"

Ray thought about it for a minute, then said, "The shooter never walked over to the body, did he, Leland?"

"That's right. I wrote it in the original crime scene report. The pictures will verify it too."

"But maybe they got scared after they realized what they had done and just ran. I mean, if they were thinking clearly, yeah, they'd go check. But they were scared, probably never killed anybody before, and ran," Ray said.

"They did run. Part of the way back at least. You can tell from the footprints," said Leland.

"They panicked, ran from the scene, and managed to calm themselves enough to make themselves walk," said Ray. He wasn't looking at either Leland or me, but staring into space like you do whenever you are trying to create a mental image of something.

" 'Course, almost anything is possible. We've seen some crazy things happen haven't we, Leland?" Ray said.

Leland nodded, but he was staring now too.

"But I think that is the most likely scenario," Ray added.

"Does make some sense," Leland said, "and that points right to one of these ranchers."

He called in a couple of his deputies, divided up his list, and gave them instructions to see what kind of tires the ranchers had on their vehicles.

"If anybody has a problem with you looking at their trucks, let me know and I'll call 'em. And whatever you do, be polite and respectful. None of these people are going to like this," Leland said. The deputies made a few notes and left.

"I didn't send them to Vernon's, figured I better do that one," he said after the deputies had gone.

"Leland, we've got to play this one straight up," Ray said.

"I know that. I'm just saying there ain't no way Vernon's gonna let anybody but me check what kind of tires he's got. He probably won't even let me. But if I send a deputy out there it'd just make it that much harder."

"Oh, I'm not worried about you checking the tires or anything like that, I'm just saying . . . well, you know . . ." Ray let his words trail off but everybody knew what he meant.

"I know, Ray, don't worry."

"I've got to get back over to my office," Ray said. "Call when you hear back from your deputies." Ray put his copy of the lab report in his briefcase, closed it, and left.

"So does this get Ty Jones off the hook?" I said after Ray had gone.

"No, not completely, but it does look less likely that he did it. Don't you think?" Leland asked.

"I would have to say so. What about the Watts girl?"

"She's not completely in the clear, but if her story continues to check out she will be soon," Leland said.

"You want to ride with me out to Vernon's place?" he added.

I didn't really want to but I felt like I should.

"You bet. You ready to go?" I said.

"Yep."

Chapter Twelve

Where Omar Blackford's house had been refined and sophisticated, Vernon's was rustic and traditional. It too was at the end of a long dirt road, but instead of appearing as though it had been picked up from an upper-class Boston neighborhood and set down in Red Creek during a tornado, Vernon's house complemented the landscape and fit into my idea of what a ranch house ought to look like.

We parked the car in front of the house and Leland knocked at the huge oak door.

"Leland, you should have called first, I would have had Mabel make us some lunch," Vernon said as he opened the door.

There are two kinds of families, one where everybody tries very hard not to offend each other, and if on a rare occasion they do then they fall all over themselves apologizing and promising to never do it again. Other families just say whatever is on their minds and let the chips fall where they may. These families often get mad and yell and argue but never feel compelled to apologize; they just forget it and move on.

Judging from what I knew of Maggie and Vernon's demeanor in answering the door, I guessed the Hansens fell into the latter category.

"No need to worry about that," Leland said. Vernon stepped aside to let us in.

"Come on back to the kitchen; we were just having some coffee," Vernon said.

We walked down a long hallway and passed a large staircase into a surprisingly small kitchen. Mabel, Vernon's wife, was wearing an apron and working at the stove. She spoke to Leland and he introduced me to her. She seemed like a friendly person and exactly the kind of woman I expected Vernon to be married to.

"Can I get you boys some coffee?" she offered.

"No, thank you," I said.

"That would be nice," Leland said.

She poured some coffee in a large cup and passed it over to Leland. Vernon passed over the cream and sugar and Leland fixed his coffee to his liking but did not drink it.

"Okay, Leland, spit it out. What did you come out here for? I can tell something's bothering you," Vernon said.

"Well, we got some of the tests back from the crime scene and it looks like it wasn't Ty's truck. So we're checking—"

"And naturally, this is the first place you come looking. I can't believe this, Leland," Vernon said, slamming his coffee cup to the table and sloshing coffee out on his hand.

"No, Vernon, this ain't the first place we came looking. But like I said the other morning, we got to check on everybody that's got a lease up there. Everybody." Leland looked Vernon in the eyes for the first time since we arrived. It was an awkward moment and I was staring at my fingernails as if I had just discovered a terminal hangnail.

Vernon returned Leland's stare for ten or fifteen seconds and finally said, "What is it you want?"

"I just need to look at your trucks, that's all."

"My trucks?"

"Yeah, your trucks. It will only take us a second and it'll probably be the last time I have to bother you about this," Leland said.

I could feel Vernon staring at me so I looked up at him. In his eyes was a mixture of frustration and anger. He stared at me for a few more seconds then looked over at Leland.

"Do whatever it is you need to do to get off of my back about this thing," Vernon said as he got up from the table and left. Mabel kept working at the stove with her back to the table as if she had heard nothing.

For a moment Leland sat at the table without saying a word, staring out the window. Finally he shook his head in disbelief, looked at me, and said, "Let's go."

Leland and I walked out the back door and followed a covered walkway to a four-car garage. Using the side door, we walked in. The sun had been so bright that it was impossible to see anything in the mostly dark garage. I could hear Leland fumbling around trying to find a light switch. Within a couple of seconds one of the garage doors began to open.

"I was looking for a light switch, but that will do, I guess," Leland said. He pulled a copy of the lab report from his pocket, unfolded it, and flipped through the pages.

Parked in Vernon's garage was a Lincoln Town Car, a Nissan Maxima, a late-model Ford truck, and in the far stall a trailer with four jet skis. Leland walked over to the truck, looked at the report, looked at the front tires, then back at the report. He followed the same procedure on the back tires without saying a word. I was wishing I had brought my copy of the report.

"Doesn't match," he said, hardly able to conceal his grin. I felt as relieved as Leland looked.

"We better go check his field trucks; I think he's got three of 'em," he said.

We got in his car and drove back down the driveway a few hundred yards and turned right on a small road I hadn't noticed on the drive in. We followed it for maybe a quarter of a mile through a field of sagebrush and scrub oaks. Vernon's house was situated in a small box canyon and the road we were following took us around the south edge of the canyon. Once out of the canyon I could see a group of three bunkhouses, a set of four or five corrals, and a huge barn. We parked by the barn where two of the trucks were parked. Both were old and beat up, rusted in a few spots and dusty inside and out.

Again Leland retrieved his copy of the report. He followed the same routine as he checked the tires.

"Not a match," he said, and turned his attention to the second truck.

He looked at the front tire, but did not look back at the report. He bent over and rubbed the dust from the tire with the back of his hand. I could not see his face, but he shook his head, stood up, and walked to the back tire, then to the other side of the truck until he had checked all four. He looked at me, then the report.

"It's a match," he said, and opened the passenger side door and slid the seat up, revealing a rifle.

"Let me guess," I said. "A .22?"

"Yep."

Leland didn't say anything for a long time. He was in a difficult situation. His brother or one of his brother's employees had just shot to the top of his suspect list.

Leland is not an indecisive person, but he can be deliberate. I noticed he had the ability to tune out the world around him and think about the situation at hand. And that was what he was doing now. His face was blank and looking out toward the horizon.

I was staring at Leland and was startled when someone yelled from the bunkhouse.

"Hey, sheriff, what you doing down here?" It was one of the ranch hands tightening up a pair of chaps with one hand and a pair of tennis shoes in the other. I didn't know that people still wore chaps, but they did apparently.

Leland just kept staring, unaware that someone was speaking to him. So I said, "We're just down here checking on some things." That satisfied him. He turned and walked back into the bunkhouse.

A second later Leland said, "Ain't but one thing to do." He walked over to his car, grabbed the mike to his CB radio, and started to say something, but stopped himself. He put the mike back in its holder and reached in the backseat to retrieve his mobile phone. He dialed a number and waited.

"Yeah, this is the sheriff. Send a tow truck out to my brother Vernon's place. Not to his house but down to the bunkhouses just south of his place."

Pause.

"That's right, about two hundred yards before you get to his house."

Pause.

"Yeah, just have 'em stay on that road till they see my car. I'll be waiting on 'em," he said, and pressed END on the phone. The noon sun was beating down on us and sweat was beading up on my neck and forehead.

"This is what you've been afraid of, I guess," he said, looking at me for the first time since he realized the tires matched the police report.

"To be honest I'd have to say yes," I said. "What happens now?"

"We'll take the truck in and confirm that it was these tires that left the tracks. Then we'll run some tests on the gun to see if it matches the bullet retrieved out of Tate's head."

"What do you think, will it match?" I said.

"The chances of having another truck with these same mismatched tires ain't very good."

"What does that mean for the investigation?"

"Depends on whose fingerprints are on the gun," he said. There was a long pause while we both considered the implication of what that meant.

"Well, I better call Vernon and let him know what's going on," he finally said, and then he started to dial his cellular.

An hour and a half later we were back in Leland's office. We had waited for the tow truck, instructed them to take Vernon's truck to the county impound, and made arrangements for the proper tests to be done on the truck and the gun. Of course, I had only been able to hear Leland's side of the conversation with Vernon, but I think, being the likely owner of the murder weapon and vehicle got Vernon's attention, he had agreed to meet Leland at his office.

"I'll tell you right now my fingerprints are on that gun. Heck, my fingerprints are on every gun I own. I drive all those trucks from time to time and I keep a .22 in all of them," Vernon said. He and I were sitting on the chairs in front of Leland's desk. Leland had been sitting at his desk, but was now up and pacing.

"What for?" I asked.

Vernon looked at me with contempt in his eyes and said, " 'Cause I run that darn ranch and I need to drive 'em."

"No, I mean why do you keep .22s in them?"

"Every once in a while we need 'em to shoot snakes or something."

"I ain't gonna lie to you, Vernon, this ain't gonna look good. Your alibi isn't that good; I can prove your truck was at the crime scene—the only vehicle the killer could have taken. In the truck was the same kind of gun that was used in the murder, and your fingerprints are all over the weapon. And you got a motive,'' Leland said.

Vernon was shaking his head. ''I don't know what to say. Maybe it was one of the ranch hands again.''

''Oh yeah, I forgot that. Threatening phone calls have been made from your ranch to the murder victim. And it was never proven who made the calls,'' Leland added.

''We both know who made those calls, Leland. And he is sitting in your jail right now,'' Vernon said.

''Yeah, but it don't matter what you and I think. Just look at what can be proved. A whole lot of things are pointing at you or at least someone who works for you.''

''Leland, anybody could have taken the truck that night. You don't even need the key to start it. All you got to do is turn the ignition and it starts just like the key was in it. All the trucks I own are that way, except for the one I drive,'' Vernon said.

''If it comes back that your gun is the murder weapon, Ray is gonna want me to arrest you, Vernon, and I don't know how I can refuse him.''

''When will you know?'' Vernon said.

''I imagine it will be Monday morning. I asked them to rush it, but I bet they won't come in on Saturday and you can forget Sunday,'' Leland said.

After Vernon had gone, Leland and I ordered sandwiches from a place just down the street from the Old Courthouse. Neither of us said much as we ate. When we finished I went to the little office I was using to call Maggie and let her know what was happening. She took the news of Vernon's truck in typical stoic fashion.

''It looks like we have another problem now,'' she said after we finished talking about Vernon.

''What?''

''I got a call from Ernie Barker over at the FBI; apparently there is a lot of talk about this murder at the Bureau,'' she said.

Ernie Barker and Maggie had been close political allies for over ten years.

"The murder was on federal land, so they have a jurisdictional hook into this thing and they're feeling some pressure. He just wanted me to know that they are watching the situation very carefully.''

"Did he say where the pressure was coming from?"

"No, he didn't have to. If you traced it back it would be coming from someone on the Senate Judiciary Committee with a tie to Montgomery,'' she said.

"Are they going to run their own investigation? In addition to Leland's?'' I asked.

"That's yet to be determined. Ernie also said that nothing was imminent and that he thought he could hold them off until after the election,'' Maggie said.

"Well, if he can do that, I don't care what the FBI does,'' I said.

"I'm still the chairperson of the Judiciary Committee. Other people can put pressure on the FBI, but as long as it looks like I still have a shot to win this election they will be very careful how they handle this one,'' she said.

"Ernie is smart enough to know what is best for us, but I told him that they should follow their normal procedure,'' she added.

"Maggie, I am not going to lie to you,'' I said. "A high-profile FBI investigation would finish us off.''

Leland was just ending a phone call when I appeared at his door and gave him my can-I-interrupt look. He motioned me in with his head. He was off the phone by the time I sat in the metal-and-vinyl chair in front of his desk. I walked him through my phone call with Maggie, explained her connection with Barker.

"No question, I'd rather not have them in here mucking around. But I am going as fast as I can right now," he said.

"You ever worked with them before?"

"Oh sure, from time to time they're interested in a case of mine," he said.

"How have they been to work with?" I asked.

"Depends on the person, really. Some of them were easy to work with, others weren't. I've never had them come and do their own investigation," he said. "I don't think I would enjoy that too much."

"I don't think any of us would," I said.

Chapter Thirteen

That night Larry Klinger had scheduled a meeting to give an update on the data collection on the yellow-backed minnow and take public comments. The meeting was held in the auditorium of Creek County High.

Creek County High School had been built in the late 1940s or 50s during the coal and uranium mining boom days. At the time, I am sure the auditorium was bigger than they ever thought they would need. But that night it seemed pitifully small and unbearably hot. I arrived a few minutes after the meeting started in order to avoid running into Hardcopy or any of the other reporters who would be covering the meeting. When I arrived, every seat was filled and I stood in the back of the auditorium with all the latecomers.

Larry had already started the meeting. He was sitting at a table in front of the stage facing the audience. He was wearing the same type uniform that he wore when I met with him in his office. I could tell he had recently had a haircut, but he also looked tired. It may have just been the bad lighting, but I noticed dark circles under his eyes that I had not noticed when I was in his office, and he frequently removed his glasses and vigorously rubbed his eyes.

"Let me conclude by saying this. Then I'll take your questions, and leave some time for public comment. The data have all been collected and are being input. I don't know what the preliminary results are, but I will know within the next two to three days. Then it will take me another two to three days before I issue a draft report.

"So that is where we are. Can I answer any questions?" Klinger said.

Before Larry had even finished his comments Omar Blackford was standing at one of three microphones set up in the front of the auditorium for the audience to use. Larry called on him to speak.

"Ah, thanks, Larry. I don't really have a question as much as I do a comment." He turned to face the audience. "Everybody here knows what's happened up in Sidewinder Canyon. I didn't always agree with Steve's tactics, none of us did, but his loss—under any conditions—is a tragedy. I started the process well over fifteen years ago, and it has become larger than any one individual or even group of individuals could handle. True, without Steve here, others and myself will have to shoulder more of the burden for finishing this job. But that's okay. Before Steve came on the scene that's the way it was going to be anyway.

"We will pick up the pieces and move on. Larry has done a good job with his research, and I am sure we are all anxious to hear what the official results are. But I am begging and pleading with everybody in this room to make a commitment to work together. I don't want to put an end to ranching in Red Creek. That's not the object of what we're trying to do here. We're trying to protect a natural heritage that belongs to all of us, all Americans.

"Are we going to have to do things differently? Yes,

yes, we probably will. But that doesn't mean the end to anybody's livelihood. Thank you.''

Omar walked to the back of the room to stand because one of the latecomers had taken his seat while he was speaking. But before he had made it to the back, someone else was speaking at another one of the microphones. I didn't recognize the man. He wore a plaid shirt, a pair of those polyester Levis, and carried a cowboy hat in his left hand.

''That's just fine and dandy for you to say, Omar. Your family already mined a fortune out of the land around here so now you want to start protecting the land. I'm tired of being lied to by the likes of you and Steve Tate. 'We don't want to end ranching.' If I have to hear another one of you self-righteous elitists say that one more time I'll be ready for a straitjacket. It's a lie, Omar, and you know it.'' He pointed his hat at Omar, but Omar just chuckled and shook his head as if he were enjoying the derision.

''Just look at what Tate was doing when he got his. Yeah, he was interested in ending ranching. I don't like to see nobody get murdered and whoever did that to Steve needs to go to jail. But just because he got murdered don't mean his motives were pure. They weren't and neither are yours, Omar.'' The cowboy finished speaking and took his seat to wild applause.

The tension hung in the room like the pall of a cheap cigar.

''Ah, let me say something here,'' Larry said. ''I cannot speak for anybody's motives but my own, but I did not join the U.S. Fish and Wildlife Service to put anybody out of work. And whatever happens I for one am committed to protecting everything I can about Red Creek, from its biological diversity to its economic stability. As for Steve Tate, I think that is in the capable hands of Sheriff Hansen.'' I could hear chuckles from a few of the environmentalists who I'm sure were not convinced that Leland was mounting a vigorous investigation to find Tate's murderer—especially since his brother was widely believed to be the lead suspect. Larry held his hand up to the audience as if to say, 'Please shut up so I can finish'.

"So let's concentrate on the issue at hand and let the sheriff do his job," Larry concluded.

The meeting went on for several more hours, but the reporters left after the first hour. They had all they needed from this meeting. Hardcopy looked like an eight-year-old who had just been handed a brand-new Sony PlayStation. I could not wait to see his story.

I had to admire Larry's patience. He listened intently to all the comments, tried to mediate as best he could, and did a good job of keeping the meeting from degenerating into a fistfight.

Chapter Fourteen

The bedroom I was sleeping in had a huge window facing east which allowed the first morning sun to sneak over the mountains to wake me with a start. I looked at the clock—7:12. That was the latest I had slept in weeks. I stumbled out of bed, made the obligatory trip to the bathroom, and headed to the kitchen. Using the microwave, I warmed some leftover coffee and was heading back to the the bedroom when out of the corner of my eye I saw something move on my couch. Startled, I dropped the scalding-hot coffee on my bare foot. I was hopping around on one foot, trying—unsuccessfully—to muffle a scream.

"Interesting way to wake up." It was Tracey, coming from the couch. I was embarrassed because I was caught in my underwear.

"What are you doing here?" I said as I beat a quick retreat to the bedroom for my pants.

"I came to go hiking," she said.

I had completely forgotten but said, "I know that, but

did you sleep here last night?'' as I hopped around the bedroom putting on my pants.

''Things were pretty hectic at the office yesterday, and I didn't make a hotel reservation,'' she was saying. I finished dressing and walked back into the family room area. She was sitting up now with a blanket wrapped around her shoulders.

''But I decided to come anyway. I mean, I figured it wouldn't be that hard to find a room,'' she continued. I noticed she was wearing one of my T-shirts. ''But I got down here about midnight and everything was taken. Finally I decided to just come over. I knocked but you didn't answer so I tried the door and it was unlocked. I tiptoed in. Hope you don't mind.''

''No, not at all,'' I said.

''You were asleep so I decided not to bother you. I found a blanket and curled up on the couch.''

''Did you forget your pajamas?'' I said, pointing to my shirt.

''No. Yes, yes I forgot them. I hope you don't mind.''

''Not at all. Anytime my wardrobe can be of service,'' I said. ''Why don't I run and pick up a paper and some coffee and you can get ready.''

When I returned with the coffee and papers she was dressed and ready for the hike.

''Smitty's got a story about Vernon's truck. There's a leak somewhere in Leland's office; Smitty knows as much as I do about it.''

''I don't know where he gets this stuff,'' Tracey said as she grabbed one of the papers and a cup of coffee. She was wearing a loose-fitting T-shirt, a pair of khaki shorts, hiking boots, and a baseball-style hat with her hair pulled into a ponytail through the hole in the back. Her legs were the lean and muscular legs of a well-conditioned athlete. My hopes of not being embarrassed were fading fast.

I left her to read the paper and drink her coffee and headed to the bathroom.

She yelled from the kitchen, "Did you see the Editorial Page?"

"No. What's on it?"

"There's an editorial about how nasty things have gotten down here. How, quote, 'politicians fan the flames with incendiary rhetoric rather than help solve the problems,' " she said.

"That sounds like it could have been written by Montgomery himself. Does it mention Maggie by name?" I yelled from the bedroom.

"Not in this one, but I'm sure that will come later," she said with a chuckle.

I finished dressing and went out to read the editorial for myself. Smitty had it all working. He had his three-part series going, he was doing a news story everyday, and he had the editorial-page editor doing his bidding as well. He had to be loving this.

I felt a little guilty about taking a day off when there was so much to be done. But it has always been my experience that when things are the most hectic a little down time focuses the mind and restores vigor. At least that's what I told myself as we drove to the trailhead. Besides, nothing more would likely happen with the investigation until the ballistic tests were complete, and that would not be until Monday or Tuesday.

The trail Tracey wanted to hike was in the Jacob Mountain range. The Jacob Mountains are a protected wilderness area, which means no mechanized vehicles. It took us about an hour to drive to the trailhead, putting us there at roughly 10:00 A.M. The Red Creek basin is a desert. Many people think of deserts in the western United States as barren wastelands. Mile after mile of sand and heat. But in reality, western deserts are among the most beautiful of all the landscapes in the world. Other climes overgrown with lush leafy trees, babbling brooks, and deep-flowing rivers almost belie their inherent dangers, but not the western landscape. A mere glance gives one the feeling of solitude, beckoning you to enjoy its wonders but to respect its power. I love being in a western desert, but I could tell I was going to love it even more while serving as Tracey's guide.

For the first several miles the trail followed a narrow canyon cut deep into the desert floor by millions upon millions of spring runoffs creating walls at least fifty feet tall and pathways less than five feet wide in some places. Eventually, the canyon began to widen and ascend into the Jacob Mountains. Gradually our altitude began to increase; with each step the slope of our climb became higher and higher. We were ascending from the desert floor onto a mountain trail. Soon the vegetation began changing from the stark desert sage to fir and cedar, with an occasional quaking aspen grove.

The coolness of the mountain air was a welcome change from the hot dry air of the desert floor. I had been able to keep pace with Tracey while the terrain was rocky and flat, but as the trail became steeper and steeper the gap widened between us.

At one point the trail opened up to an expansive vista over the Red Rock Basin and the Lower Jacob Mountains. Tracey stopped there and waited for me to catch up.

"There are not too many places back east that you can see this far," she said when I caught up.

"There are not many places anywhere where you can see this far," I said.

"Should we have lunch here so we can enjoy this view?" she said.

I looked at my watch; it was already 1:10. I didn't want to stop because I knew my leg muscles would tighten and make the rest of the climb that much more difficult. But I did not want to use that as an excuse and unfortunately could not think of another good reason why we should keep moving.

"Sounds great," I said, realizing again the power of vanity.

We were carrying our lunches in trail-size fanny packs, which we removed from our waists and set on a large rock. Tracey positioned herself on the same rock in such a way that she could continue to enjoy the panoramic view.

We dug our lunches out of our bags and started eating. Tracey was breathing slightly heavier than normal and her body was covered with a thin layer of perspiration, giving her tan skin an engaging allure. I watched her—enjoying the view, eating her apple—and realized I couldn't take my eyes off her. It was one of those surreal moments in which you are able to look at someone you know quite well from a new perspective. I had always thought of Tracey as a tough-minded professional—always professional. But there, sitting on that rock, unaware of my gaze, she seemed to change from the two-dimensional personality I had known at the office into a three-dimensional person. I could suddenly see her playing hopscotch in grade school, on a high school basketball team, graduating from college, driving home for Thanksgiving dinner, breaking up with a boyfriend, reading a book in the park, arguing with her parents. I could see the whole person. Not the one you get to know working in the same office with someone—not just the sum of the parts, but the parts themselves.

I just sat there and stared at her for I don't know how long.

"You better eat your lunch," she said, startling me from my daze. "We can't sit here all afternoon."

"Oh yeah, I was just, ah, resting," I said, wondering if she had noticed me staring at her. She gave no indication that she had.

I fished around in my fanny pack for a sandwich and she

went back to enjoying the view. Within a couple of minutes we had finished our lunches and were headed up the trail again. I had been right about my leg muscles—they were aching and stiff. But I was much too proud to say anything about it and did the best I could to keep up.

My heart was pumping and my legs quivering when we reached the summit of our hike. Tracey had been admiring the view for four or five minutes when I finally hobbled to the crest.

A few hundred yards below us opened a small valley that looked like it had been carved out of the mountaintop with a giant ice cream scoop. In the center of the small valley was a lake of clear blue water. Although a slight breeze blew where we were standing, the lake was perfectly calm and looked more like a mirror than a body of water. Around the lake was a meadow of wild flowers and a grove of quaking aspen, just beginning to turn yellow with the crisp autumn air.

I had caught up to Tracey as she enjoyed the view but I could not help myself any longer. I bent over, placed a hand on each knee, and tried as best I could to catch my breath.

"It's like a hidden paradise tucked away up here," she said and was on her way down to the lake before I could manage a reply. I took a few minutes to catch my breath and followed.

I found Tracey sitting in the meadow of flowers eating an apple.

"I thought you said you liked hiking," she said as I caught up to her.

"I like it, but I don't get a chance to do it that often," I said between breaths. I checked my watch; it was already two o'clock and I was beginning to worry about whether we would get back before dark. But I was too tired to think about going back without resting.

I lay back and must have closed my eyes and gone to sleep. When I awoke Tracey was gone. I bolted straight up and looked around. She was sitting by the lake retying her shoes. I took a minute to collect my thoughts and let the sleep fade from my eyes. When I tried to move my body refused. I could not believe I was only halfway done with this hike. And I could not believe that I was stupid enough to let myself go to sleep and let my muscles tighten even more. But once again my vanity got the better of me and I willed myself to my feet and began walking. I must have been borne a remarkable resemblance to Frankenstein.

"Are you okay?" Tracey yelled from the lakeshore.

"Oh yeah, fine. Back's just a little stiff," I lied.

"What do they call this lake?" she said.

"Mirror Lake," I said. "The way this valley is situated it hardly ever gets much wind and the lake is usually really smooth like a mirror."

"It's absolutely breathtaking. It's like a painting or an Ansel Adams photograph. Look at the way those mountains are perfectly reflected in the water. Remarkable. If you took a picture of just the reflection, no one would believe it was a reflection," she said.

"There are a lot of beautiful places in the West like this," I said, taking a deep breath of the cool mountain air. "You should take some time off next spring and do some serious hiking out here. You'd love it."

"If it is anything like this I *would* love it," she said.

Eventually I got my legs and back reasonably limbered up and we made our way back down the mountainside and through the canyon. As our car came into sight I realized that I had not thought about the campaign since I left the car this morning. It was the longest I had gone without thinking about the campaign in months. I felt guilty but refreshed.

"You're not going to try to drive back tonight, are you?" I said.

"I was planning on it, but I thought we would get done earlier than this," she said, looking at her watch.

"Why don't you stay and head back in the morning?" I said.

"Do you think I can get a room tonight?" she said.

"No, but you can use the bed and I'll take the couch if that doesn't bother you," I said, knowing that obviously it didn't.

"It doesn't bother me, if you are okay with it," she said, and gave me that almost-imperceptible wink she has.

"It seemed to work out fine last night," I said as we reached the car and I unlocked the doors. "I ought to start charging rent. Besides, it will give you a chance to experience the Creek Side Café, and no trip to Red Creek is complete without that."

Chapter Fifteen

The next morning I exhausted all of my willpower forcing my aching legs and back out of bed. The previous day's hike—or death march, as I now considered it—was exacting its toll. I stumbled around the house looking for Tracey, but she was not to be found. I hoped she had gone for coffee and newspapers. I took about two Advil and slipped into a steaming-hot bath to soak my back and legs.

I must have closed my eyes and dozed back to sleep, because the next thing I remember is hearing Tracey come in the front door. She checked the bedroom and, seeing I was not in bed, called out for me.

"I'm in the bath," I yelled back.

She grabbed the bathroom doorknob and jiggled it as if she were going to come in. I shot up out of the bathtub and grabbed the only towel in the bathroom to cover myself. I must have made a terrible commotion, because I could hear Tracey laughing on the other side of the door.

"Relax, hotshot, I'm not coming in," she said. "I got some hot coffee and a copy of the *Sunday Times*."

I had to laugh too. "I'll be out in a second."

In my panic, I had accidentally dipped about half of the towel in the tub, making it difficult to dry off. I slipped into my bedroom, dressed in jeans and a T-shirt, and then tried to join Tracey in the kitchen without walking like a ninety-year-old stroke victim.

She was already sipping her coffee and engrossed in the *Times*. I grabbed my coffee and paper and sat across the table from her and started reading without a word. I could not help thinking about how strange it was to be in this house with Tracey, on a Sunday morning, reading the Sunday newspaper, enjoying a cup of hot coffee.

It was strange, yet strangely comfortable.

Tracey's hair was pulled back into a tight ponytail which brushed her shoulders. She was wearing a pair of jean shorts, sandals, and a tan T-shirt with a Nike swoosh plastered across the front. She was completely absorbed in the newspapers, her eyes bright and focused, contemplating every word. I don't know why, but I felt like laughing. Just then she noticed me staring at her.

"What are you doing?" she said. A hint of smile appeared around her eyes.

"Just watching you read," I said, feigning innocence.

"What's so funny?" she said.

"Nothing. Just the way you are consumed by the story, hanging on every word."

"Well, we've got a lot riding on this story. I'm interested," she said a little more defensively than I was prepared for.

"I know, I know I'm probably worse than you are. I mean, I wake up two or three times a night worrying about what's going to be in the *Capitol Times* in the morning," I said.

"I do the same thing. Disgusting, isn't it?" she said.

We finished the paper and walked over to the Creek Side. It was a cool day and for the first time I could feel autumn in the air. The sky was cloudless and a deep blue, a breeze was blowing out of the canyon. If my legs and back had not been killing me I might have been enjoying myself, but I could barely put one foot in front of the other. We stopped at a newspaper vending machine and bought two copies of the *Red Creek Reporter* to read over breakfast.

The Creek Side was extremely busy and we had to wait ten or fifteen minutes to get a table. But as usual, it was worth the wait. Tracey loved it. She must have eaten half her body weight in pancakes and hash browns.

"Don't take this the wrong way," I said, "but you eat a lot."

"Yeah," she said, as if to say "what's your point?"

"How do you stay so . . . so trim?" I said, stammering for the right word.

"Exercise. I jog about seventy to eighty miles a week," she said. The muscles in my legs started quivering at the mere mention of seventy miles.

"If I ate as much as you I'd be as big around as I am tall," I said.

She laughed. "I used to be fifty pounds over-weight."

I felt my jaw hit my chest.

"No, it's true. When I was in high school I was chunky, but then when I got to college—especially while I was interning in D.C.—I really started putting on weight. I had three complete wardrobes. Finally I got sick of always being tired, so I lost thirty pounds and got back into my smallest wardrobe. I was back down to my high school weight. It was great. But when I went off the diet I gained it right back," she said.

"Then I read an article in *The New York Times* by some doctor who said you could eat anything you wanted if you got enough exercise. I started jogging that day. Within a year I had lost the first thirty pounds and within two years I lost another twenty and had worked my way up to ten miles a day. And the article was right, if you get enough exercise you can eat just about anything you want.''

We finished eating and Tracey left for Wasatch City. I spent the day answering my e-mail, talking with Mike on the phone, and refining the questionnaire for our poll. Leland called about three-thirty and invited me to dinner at six. I accepted the offer and had an enjoyable evening at his place. I returned to the house at nine-thirty, called Maggie, and gave her an update. About eleven-thirty I went to bed still tired and and sore from the hike.

Monday morning's *Capitol Times* story was the second part in the three-part series. Where the first part had told about Omar Blackford and the beginnings of the Red Creek environmental movement, the second told the story of Steve Tate and the MountainLand Liberation Front.

It read in part:

> . . . Tate was a flamboyant leader who understood that the Red Creek movement needed ''a face.'' A strong personality that could not only energize the faithful, but also draw on the financial resources the national environmental groups brought to the southern Utah town.
>
> His style, which alienated him from most longtime Red Creek residents, overshadowed many of the long-suffering environmentalists who originally brought Red Creek to the attention of the national movement.
>
> Tate often used controversial and sometimes illegal tactics, refusing to compromise when he felt like victory was at hand.
>
> He first came to Red Creek in 1982 at the invitation of Omar Blackford, the father of southern Utah's en-

vironmental movement. After the initial visit, he returned often for extended visits until finally making Red Creek his permanent home or "base of operations"—as Tate was known to say—in the fall of 1988. . . .

After finishing the paper, I spent the rest of the morning on conference calls with the campaign staff and returning phone calls. I talked to Maggie for about ten minutes, spent about half an hour on the phone with our pollster finalizing the questions for our survey, and another five minutes with Tracey.

I had not spoken with Smitty for several days and thought I had better give him a call. I dialed the number and waited on hold for a minute or so.

"Smitty," he said by way of salutation.

"Smitty, Sam. I haven't talked with you for a couple of days so I thought I'd better call and find out where to send the flowers."

"Flowers?"

"For your funeral," I said. "It's been so long I thought you must have died a sudden death."

"I'm telling you, a couple of stiff drinks every evening about five-thirty offsets any damage caused by cigarettes and a bad diet," Smitty said as if he really believed it.

"Words to live by," I said. "Anything new?"

"I was just about to call you. Montgomery is really gearing up on this environmental stuff. Saying the senator is part of the problem." He made a statement but his voice inflections sounded as though he was asking a question. This was a technique that Smitty often used.

"Does that surprise you, Smitty?" I asked. I always try to make him ask me a specific question rather than just commenting on what he says.

"No." He chuckled. "But I can't imagine that you guys

had planned on closing the campaign talking about the environment. Did you?''

''Well, you never really know how a campaign is going to close. But Senator Hansen has an environmental record that she is proud of. And we have something that Jeff doesn't have.''

''What's that?''

''A record of delivering for this state. On environmental and other issues. Jeff has done nothing but stand on the sidelines and criticize the efforts of others. So if he wants to talk about who has done what for Utah—let's go.''

''It's amazing how you can say that with so much conviction. It's almost like you really believe it,'' Smitty said. I could here the smile in his voice.

''I do mean it,'' I said with even more conviction.

''I suppose it won't surprise you that I've been taking a close look at the senator's record. Environmental record, I mean.''

''No, I'm not surprised.''

''There's some good stuff in there to be sure, but when you dig deep enough there is quite a bit in there that isn't going to sell so well in Wasatch City.''

This was where I had to be really careful. ''I don't think there is any question that when the people of this state examine the senator's record in its entirety, they will find that she has always acted in the best interest of the state.''

''Of course Montgomery isn't going to lay her entire record before the people,'' Smitty said.

''No, I wouldn't expect him to be that fair-minded. But we will and we are confident that the people will agree with us,'' I said

''At any rate, it's going to be fun to watch,'' Smitty said, enjoying my pain. ''I'm working on a story—probably run tomorrow—kind of chronicling the senator's record. I worked on it all weekend; it's pretty long.''

"I can't wait to read it," I said, trying to keep the dread out of my voice.

"It isn't that bad. Call me if anything comes up."

"You'll be the first I call," I said, and hung up.

It was late in the morning before I got a call from Tracey.

"Jackson Kidrick's office just called for you, they want you to call them," she said.

Jack Kidrick is one of Maggie's oldest and most faithful supporters, going back to her days in the state legislature. He is also one of Utah's leading citizens. Very wealthy, he got rich as an entrepreneur starting and selling—for huge profits—several high-tech companies. Since then, he had diversified interests and has had his hand in almost everything from land development to aerospace to power generation. So in short, Jack Kidrick gets his calls returned.

"What does he want?" Tracey said.

"I don't know, but he doesn't call to chitchat."

I immediately called the offices of Kidrick Capital and got Jack's assistant. He sounded like a young kid fresh out of some MBA program somewhere.

"Yes, Mr. Kidrick told me you might be calling. Unfortunately, he is at a business meeting in Dallas," said the young assistant.

"I'm sorry I missed him. Do you know what it might have been regarding?" I said, still curious.

"He has asked if you could join him for a round of golf at the country club in the morning about ten o'clock. Are you available?" he said.

"Yes, I can be there." Like I said, for Jack Kidrick I am always available.

"Very well, sir. It's ten then. Are you aware of the dress code at the country club?"

"Yes, I'll make a note to leave my cutoffs and tank top at home," I said.

Jack Kidrick really had my attention. I had met him on many occasions and had talked to him on the phone numerous times over the last few years. Although he was always very polite and courteous, none of those conversations lasted more than five minutes and were very businesslike—no time wasted on small talk. But tomorrow I would have an audience with him for three or four hours—at his request.

I decided to take the next flight to Wasatch City and spend the afternoon in the campaign office. I made the reservation and called Tracey to meet me at the airport.

Chapter Sixteen

When I saw Tracey at the airport, she was holding a videotape in her hand. I have no idea why she brought it with her since there was no place at the airport we could view it.

"Montgomery has his new ads up," she said by way of greeting.

"What do they say?" I asked as I dropped my carry-on bag and grabbed the videotape as if holding the tape would give me some special insight.

"It's Montgomery talking about the natural beauty of the state and how it is time to heal our state. Blah blah blah. It's pretty good," she said.

We hurried to the campaign office and viewed the ad. It was a good spot and Montgomery looked great on TV. But more important, the ad touched on an issue that resonated with a lot of people in Utah—people are sick of all the fighting over the environment. People are ready to move beyond the arguing to solve the outstanding problems. And

Montgomery did a very good job of playing on those sentiments.

Tracey and I watched the ad several times without making comments.

After the third viewing I said, "You were right, it is a good ad. It goes right to the heart of our problem but without a direct attack on Maggie. It's very good. When did it start running?"

"First thing this morning," Tracey said.

"How big is the buy?"

"I don't think they have bought any new time, but they have pulled all their old spots and are running this one instead."

"Well, this one is going to hurt. Has Maggie seen it?"

"I called her at home this morning before she left for her appointments and told her about it, but I don't think she has seen it yet," Tracey said.

"Maybe that's for the best. Let's try to decide how we're going to respond to this thing before she has a chance to see it," I said.

I asked Nina to send out for some dinner and to get our media consultants on the phone.

We spent the rest of the afternoon and evening working on a response ad. Although it was not nearly as good as Montgomery's I thought that it was the best that we could do. Our ad talked about all the environmental issues Maggie had helped resolve and her commitment to preserving the pristine areas of our state while balancing legitimate economic concerns. The media team would take the red-eye from Washington and be in Wasatch City in the morning to shoot the ad.

As if on cue Maggie walked into the conference room just as we were finishing our work.

"Okay. Let's see this ad. It is all I heard about all day.

Everywhere I go,'' she said as she took the seat at the head of the conference table.

We rewound the ad and played it for her. This time I did not watch the ad—I watched Maggie. Her face was intense, but seemed almost indifferent. When the ad ended she stared at the blank screen thoughtfully for just a second or two.

Then she looked at me and asked, ''So how do we respond?''

I went over with her all the work we had done that afternoon and evening so that she would understand why we decided to take the course we were recommending.

''I thought you would be more negative,'' she said. I could tell from her body language that she was relieved that we weren't suggesting it now.

''Normally I would, but they did a pretty good job boxing us in. I'm sure you noticed that they did not even mention your name. So if we come out after him directly, it is going to look like were are overreacting.''

''I can see that,'' she said. ''I like this approach. When do we shoot?''

Later that same night, I was in my office eating a bag of chips and checking my e-mail when I got a call from Smitty.

''I guess it was inevitable,'' he said.

''What's that?''

''This Montgomery ad for one thing.''

''Yeah, I think it's a shame when politicians try to capitalize on a tragedy,''

''You don't think an ad talking about his approach on environmental issues is appropriate?'' Smitty asked.

''I'll leave it to the voters to decide what is appropriate. But if this is such an important issue for Montgomery, why did it take a murder to get him to talk about it?''

''I can see how you would see it that way. I can also

see how some people—maybe a lot of people—would see it Montgomery's way.''

''That's why they hold elections,'' I said

''Anything else you want to say on this?'' Smitty asked.

''No. Not really,'' I said, feeling completely helpless.

''Sammy, there's a lot of stuff going on under the radar, so to speak. You know what I mean?'' Smitty said. I could tell he was holding the phone closer to his lips and speaking more softly than normal.

''Yeah,'' I said without a clue what he was talking about. I kept my answer short hoping it would draw more out of him.

''I'm going to tell you something else. I don't think you guys are looking at all the angles.''

''What do you mean?'' I asked. Because if there was one thing I knew, it was that Smitty knew how to look at all the angles.

''Just what I said. Sometimes the right answer isn't the most obvious. That's all.''

''Do you know something I don't?'' I said.

''Look, just think about what I said. Call me if you hear anything,'' he said, and hung up before I had a chance to say anything else.

Smitty, I believed, was trying to tell me something. He had a theory or something of that nature. If he knew something for a fact, he would act on it, probably by writing a story. I thought and thought, but I couldn't figure what message he was trying to send me. It could have been about the murder, or it could have been about the campaign. He knew I was too emotionally invested to look at either the campaign or the murder objectively. But he had noticed something I had not. Something that was not very obvious.

I thought about the murder and rehearsed in my mind everything I knew about it. As I had originally feared, a lot of evidence seemed to be pointing at Vernon being involved at some level. But Smitty had said that sometimes the most obvious answer is not the right answer. I tried to rethink the whole thing. What possible motives could anyone have had to kill Tate? Although I knew I could have been missing something, in the end, I couldn't figure it out.

Next, my thought turned to the campaign. Was there some subtle undercurrent that I was missing? Had I been spending so much time on this murder that I was missing something else just as important? I went over and over it in my mind but came up with nothing.

When I next looked at my watch it was 11:45. I was ready to go home and get in my own bed for a change. I finished responding to all my e-mails and locked up the office. I was halfway to my parking place when I realized that I had left my car at the apartment. I turned around and went back in the office to call a cab. When I walked in I was startled to see Tracey was still at her desk working.

"What are you still doing here?" I asked.

She jumped. "I thought you left," she said, holding her hand to her heart as if she were trying to calm herself.

"I did leave. But I realized I don't have a car here. So I came in to call a cab."

"Oh, don't do that. I was just leaving and I can drop you off," she said.

"Are you sure it's not too much trouble?" I asked.

"No. No problem at all."

"What are you still doing here?" I said.

"Just trying to make final arrangements for the shoot tomorrow. I never realized what really goes into these commercials. It is hard to throw a shoot together in twelve hours. I've got to be out there at four-thirty tomorrow morning," she said as she turned her computer off and grabbed her purse.

I turned off her lights and we were on our way.

We drove in silence. I thought how nice it was that our relationship had matured to the point that silence was not awkward. I did not feel the need to say anything, and apparently, neither did she.

Again my thoughts turned to my earlier conversation with Smitty. I thought of telling Tracey what he had said, but decided to keep it to myself.

Instead I asked, "What are we missing here, Tracey? What are we overlooking?"

"Like what?" she said, glancing at me.

"I don't know. Is there something happening in this campaign that maybe an outsider might see that we could have missed?"

She thought for a long time before saying, "I'm too tired to really think right now, but nothing really comes to mind. Why do you ask?"

"No reason in particular," I lied. "But sometimes you can't see the forest for the trees. I just think we need to take a step back and look around, just to make sure we are not missing anything," I said.

"I don't want to carry this analogy too far, but I am so far into this forest, all I can see is trees. You know what I mean? With this shoot tomorrow and everything, that's all I've got time to think about. Is there something specific that is bothering you?"

"No. Not really. Just nervous paranoia, I guess," I said, rubbing my temples.

"I don't have time to be paranoid. You're on your own with that one," she said. And we slipped back into silence.

Chapter Seventeen

I woke up the next morning at my usual time. My head-ache was gone and it was a perfect day for golfing. But I could not get really excited about it. I had too many other things on my mind to be golfing, but when Jack Kidrick wants to golf—you golf.

I pulled on a jogging suit and walked over to the coffee-house and bought a newspaper and a cup of coffee. The third part of Smitty's three-part series was on the first page below the fold. The headline read: HANSEN A CHAMELEON ON ENVIRONMENT. As usual it was a fair and balanced story, pointing out the perceived inconsistencies in Mag-gie's record. Talking in excruciating detail about some of the positions Maggie had taken as a new senator, complete with some of her old quotes about the environmental move-ment. But to his credit, he spent an equal amount of time talking about the Jacob Mountain Wilderness Area bill that Maggie had passed. In fact, the story showed that, like many of her constituents, Maggie's views on environmental issues had evolved over the years. The problem is that most people do not recognize when their opinions are shifting and probably would not recognize it in their elected representatives unless people like Smitty pointed it out to them. All in all, I thought the story was a net benefit to the Montgomery campaign, but at the same time, I could not argue with anything in it.

I arrived at the Wasatch Country Club properly attired at nine-thirty and went straight to the driving range. I had not played golf in three months and I did not want to embarrass myself in front of Jack Kidrick.

The leaves were changing and it was just cool enough to be comfortable in a golf shirt and sweater. I hit a large bucket of balls, loosened up my back, and met Jack at the first tee a few minutes before ten.

Jack Kidrick is tall—about six four—with an athletic build. Contray to most people with his kind of wealth and power, he always seems approachable and friendly.

"Hi, Sam. It is good to see you again," he said as soon as he saw me.

"Thanks for inviting me, Jack. How are you?" I said, shaking his outstretched hand.

"I'm fine. Glad you could make it." He walked over to the tee box.

"Listen," he said, "I hope you don't mind, but it's just going to be you and me today."

"I don't mind at all. Isn't it a great day for golf?" I asked as we were met by our two caddies.

Jack took his driver and teed up his ball. My caddy handed me my driver as I waited my turn.

Just as he was about to begin his windup, Jack stopped and asked me, "How about a game of ten ten ten?"

"Sounds good," I said. In other words we had ten dollars on the first nine holes, ten dollars on the second nine holes, and ten dollars on the eighteenth hole. I was hoping I had thirty dollars on me, because I had a feeling I was about to lose.

I played better than I expected and I was able to take my mind off the campaign and the murder for a while and really enjoy myself. Jack and I were about the same handicap, which kept the round competitive and in the end I only owed him twenty dollars. It would have been thirty, but by some unexplainable miracle I chipped the ball in from thirty yards out on the eighteenth hole for a birdie.

Jack never brought up any business while we were golfing. He asked me questions about my life, where had I grown up, where I went to college, how I had come to work for Maggie. In turn he told me about himself, how he got started in business, where his lucky breaks had been. We talked about golf courses we had played and courses we would like to play. But through the whole round he never gave me any hint why I was invited to play golf that day. We just enjoyed a round of golf.

When we finished I settled up with Jack and he used his winnings to tip the caddies.

"I hope you can join me for a little lunch," he said.

"I'd love to."

We found a table on the patio outside the main dining room overlooking the eighteenth hole. As soon as we were seated, our waiter came over and took our drink orders. I had a Diet Coke with a twist of lime and Jack ordered a scotch.

"You're probably wondering why I've wasted so much of your time today," Jack said after the waiter had left.

"Believe me, it has not been a waste of time. But you have piqued my curiosity," I answered.

"Well, let's cut to the chase," he said. "About ten or eleven years ago I bought a construction company that specializes in building power generation plants not only in this country, but all over the world.''

I nodded my head. That much I already knew.

''For the last three and a half years I have been working on a deal to build three power plants in central and southern China,'' he continued. ''As you can imagine it is a very big deal. We are talking about tens of billions of dollars. I think we are going to close this deal, but we are at least ten to twelve months away. And there are still plenty of things that could kill it. You know how it is.''

I nodded even though I had very little understanding of the world Jack Kidrick lived in.

''Senator Hansen's help has been critical so far. She has used her contacts in the State Department to open doors for us that I did not even know existed. I mean, without her, I doubt we would even be in the game.''

I had been aware of this project. I also knew that Maggie had made several phone calls for Jack and on at least three occasions I could think of, she had personally set up meetings between State Department and Chinese officials for Jack.

''Frankly, because of the success we have had, I've poured literally millions of dollars into this project, all of which will be lost if we don't get the bid. Do you understand?'' he asked and paused, waiting for a response from me.

''Yes, it sounds very dicey,'' I said.

''Here is what makes me nervous,'' he said, looking me straight in the eye. ''One of the things that could kill this bid quicker than anything I can think of is a hostile U.S. senator. One or two phone calls to the State Department and this deal could implode real quick.''

''Jack, you don't have anything to worry about. Senator Hansen would never in a million years do anything like that.'' But even as I was saying it, I realized he wasn't worried about Senator Hansen, he was worried about Senator Montgomery.

"I understand that, but what about Jeff Montgomery?" he said and paused for a minute while I caught up with him.

"I still think Maggie is going to win this election," Jack said. "But if we are being honest, with everything that is going on in Red Creek, we have to acknowledge the fact that Montgomery has a decent chance of pulling the upset. Do you disagree?"

I wanted so badly to disagree, but I couldn't and maintain any credibility with Jack. He had probably done his own polling and knew what was happening in this race.

"No, I don't disagree, Jack. But we are still the front-runner in this race and we still have more money than he does. Maggie is going to win. But even so, if Montgomery did win, it would be suicide for him to kill your deal." Some people were just too big to be pushed around and Jack Kidrick was one of them.

"I think she'll win too, but her support is softening. Things in Red Creek could go from bad to worse at any minute," Jack said.

"I'm keeping a close watch on what's going on in Red Creek. And I really don't think anything is going to happen down there until well after the election," I said.

"The fact that they haven't arrested anyone and, as you say, won't until after the election is a big part of the problem. Even I am starting to believe that Leland is covering for Vernon. At least until this election is over," he said, looking over a pair of reading glasses and right into my eyes.

I started to respond, but out of the corner of my eye I saw our waiter approaching with our drink order. He served our drinks and we ordered lunch. I ordered a club sandwich even though I had completely lost my appetite.

"I have seen and heard all the evidence in that case," I

said after the waiter had left "and some of it points to Vernon, but there is nothing conclusive, Jack. And this much I know for sure, I would not be involved in any kind of a cover-up."

"Listen, Sam. Let me bottom line this for you. One thing I cannot afford is a hostile U.S. senator. And we both know that Montgomery is petty enough to kill this deal out of nothing more than spite if he felt like his fingerprints would not be on it," he said.

I had to acknowledge that was true.

"So what I'm going to do is buy a table at Montgomery's fund-raiser on Friday. My wife, all my executives, and I have maxed out our contributions to Senator Hansen's campaign and our support still lies with her. But this one contribution will cover me with Montgomery if he wins," Jack said, and waited for my response.

I could not really argue with anything he said. I was sure that if I were in his shoes I would do the same thing he was doing. But this was a bad omen. Even Hardcopy could figure this one out and it would be one more sign that Maggie was in trouble. Sitting where I was, if I looked way off into the distance, I could see the vultures beginning to circle.

But we weren't dead yet.

"Jack," I finally said. "You have got to do what you think is best, and I really can't argue with your reasoning. But you understand that this will hurt Senator Hansen and help Montgomery."

"I know. I have anguished over this all week. But in the end, this is what I need to do." He paused. "When we leave here today I am going to call Maggie and tell her what I have just told you. I wanted you to know first, because I am hopeful that you can take a more dispassionate view of it than the senator will be able to. In any event I hope you will allow me to speak to her first."

I thought about trying to change his mind, but I could see it was useless.

"I'll wait to hear from her. She will call me the minute she hangs up with you," I said.

"If there is any thing I can do to lessen the impact in the media I will be happy to do whatever I can," he said.

"I'm sure some reporters are going to call you. It would help if you tell them you're still endorsing Senator Hansen," I said.

"That will not be a problem; I had decided to do that in any event. Oh, one other thing. I really think a lot of you, Sam, and if you ever decide to leave the senator I would like to put you to work in my organization somewhere," he said.

"That's very kind of you," I said as our lunches arrived.

I forced down my club sandwich and excused myself. This, I was sure, must have been what Smitty was referring to in our conversation the night before. He must be catching wind of this. When people like Jack Kidrick start shifting political alliances it means something. In this case it was a clear sign that Maggie was in trouble. We were doing all we could, but I wasn't sure whether it was going to be enough.

I went to the office to wait for Maggie's phone call. It was an utterly helpless feeling.

Chapter Eighteen

Two hours after my lunch with Jack Kidrick I was sitting in my office staring out the window when Maggie's call came through.

"Sam, I just had a very disturbing phone call from Jack Kidrick," she said. I could clearly hear the anger in her voice, but the panic I expected was missing. And strangely enough that made me feel a little better.

"I had the same conversation with him early this afternoon," I said.

"Why didn't you call me? You know I hate being surprised by phone calls like that," she said as the anger rose in her voice.

What could I say? She was right. I don't know what I was thinking.

"I'm sorry. He asked me to wait," I mumbled.

"Sam! Who do you work for, him or me?" she said.

"You're right, you're right. I am sorry. I was just stunned, I guess."

"Oh, all right. Don't worry about it. I might have done the same thing. Who knows," she said. I could hear her removing her earring.

"Smitty's already gotten wind of this or something like it," I said. "He tried to warn me on the phone last night, but what he said was so cryptic I didn't understand. You know how he can be sometimes."

"What did he say?" she asked.

"Just that there was 'a lot of stuff going on under the radar.' "

"Sounds to me like this might just be the tip of the iceberg," she said.

"Unfortunately I think you're right," I said.

"Sam. What's wrong with you?" she said, the anger again rising in her voice. "I am not rolling over for these guys. I have already told you I do not intend to lose due to a scandal. We've got to fight back. You can't roll over now, Sam."

Maggie was no quitter, I knew that. But I am embarrassed to admit that I had forgotten what a fighter she is. Her previous election campaigns that I had been involved with had all been big wins. Each time she got over sixty percent of the vote. I was being soft and Maggie made it clear that that was unacceptable. She was not afraid of guys like Jack Kidrick and she was not afraid to fight back. I drew strength from her strength and decided it was time to go on the offensive.

Montgomery had been in the state legislature in the 1970s when it was in vogue to oppose the death penalty and he had made some bad votes. I had seen the research, but not paid it much attention because I could not imagine ever being in a situation where we would need to use it. But here we were.

I called Mike into my office and had him pull all of our opposition research. He was back in my office in ten minutes with four three-ring binders—everything you ever wanted to know about Jefferson Montgomery. I quickly turned to the tab marked STATE LEGISLATURE 1975–78. There it was. Exactly one vote every year for four years against the death penalty. And, as an added bonus in his final year as a legislator he was the bill's chief sponsor. All the research was there in black and white.

I called our media consultants who were still in town and got them busy working on a new ad featuring Mr. Montgomery and his record on the death penalty. Within thirty-six hours he was going to be spending at least some of his precious campaign resources explaining why he believed the death penalty is "nothing more than state-sponsored murder."

The old adage that the best offense is a good defense does not hold up in politics. In fact, the converse is true, the best defense is a good offense. That death penalty ad would get us out of a defensive mode and into an offensive mode, but even so I still held out our hope that something might break our way in Red Creek. Things were bad in Red Creek; Jack Kidrick had summed it up pretty well. But before I completely wrote the whole thing off to an absolute disaster, I wanted to make one trip down there. I had Nina book me on the five-thirty flight to Red Creek. I would give it another twenty-four hours to see if anything would break, and after that I had to stop worrying about it and worry about how we were going to win in spite of it. I did not want to even think about that, but it looked as though I was going to have to face up to it.

I made it to the plane just as they were starting to shut the door. The gate attendant let me squeeze through and I found my seat. A few minutes later the wheels were up.

* * *

I was starving when we landed in Red Creek so I rented a car and headed for the Creek Side Café. When I arrived, the place was completely full as usual. I noticed Larry Klinger about halfway through a chicken sandwich. I walked over and asked if I could join him.

"Sure," he said. His eyes looked tired, but his smile was warm and genuine. "I'd like the company."

"How's business?" I asked.

"I'm trying to finish the biological survey on the yellow-backed minnow and it is about to kill me," he said.

"That's a lot of work, I guess," I said as I absentmindedly looked through a menu.

"A ton. I've been begging my supervisor up in Wasatch City to send me some help, but she says they can't spare anybody. If it weren't for Omar, I don't know what I'd do."

"Omar?" I said.

"Yeah, he volunteers his time helping me. He's the only help I've got," he said.

The waitress came and took my order and after she had gone I asked, "What's it looking like?"

"I can't really say anything. But this much I can promise you—a lot of people are going to be mad," he said, leaning across the table to tell me as if he were revealing some big secret.

"Imagine they are," I said with just a touch more sarcasm in my voice than I had intended.

"I'm serious," he said, leaning back into his seat. "You watch, this thing is going to cause shock waves from here to the East Coast. I'm telling you."

It was clear to me that Larry needed a vacation, so I changed the subject as gracefully as I could. We chatted about family and colleges while he finished his sandwich and I waited on mine. When he finished eating, he grabbed his briefcase and a huge armload of file folders and headed for the door.

I ate alone thinking again about the golf game with Jack Kidrick and my conversation with Smitty the night before. One statement kept repeating in my head over and over again. *"Sometimes the obvious answer isn't the right answer."* I began to think that he was referring more to the murder than the campaign. There must be some angle I was missing. I was convinced that he had taken an angle on this thing that no one had thought of yet. But what it was, I had no idea.

I sat there for anther twenty minutes or so going over what I knew about Steve Tate's murder. Everything about it pointed to Vernon or someone who worked for Vernon. I was tempted to call Smitty and ask him to explain himself but decided against it. Within a minute or two Wilma brought my check. I left a twenty-dollar bill to cover the check and a good tip since I didn't plan on being back for a while, then got up to leave. As I did, I noticed a bright green computer disk on the seat where Larry had been sitting. The disk was marked DATA—BACKUP. I tucked the disk into my own briefcase, thinking that Larry must have accidentally left it and that I would return it to him. It was a beautiful evening. I decided to walk the three and a half blocks to the Fish and Wildlife office where I was sure Larry would be working.

It was just getting dark as I approached the single-story office. I could see that most of the lights were still on, but Larry's old truck was the only one in the parking lot.

I was still twenty or thirty yards away when I saw a blinding light and a split second later I felt a deafening blast. I realized I was no longer standing, but lying on my back, with my left foot bent awkwardly under me. There was searing pain over my left eye. Something wet was leaking on my face.

I remember being confused as darkness gathered around me—slowly at first but then quickly, until all I could see was a faint light directly over me, but a long way off in the distance. And then that too went dark.

Chapter Nineteen

The next thing I became aware of was a television mounted on a wall. Even though I was not really trying to think, everything seemed confused. I moved my head to see where I was and a pain shot down my forehead I will never forget.

"Don't try to move," said a female voice from behind me. I heard a door open and the same female said in a louder voice, "He's waking up. Call the doctor."

My mind began clearing somewhat and I recognized the voice as Tracey's asking the nurse to please hurry. I wanted to turn my head to see her, but I did not dare move my head again. Soon enough she walked into my field of vision.

"How do you feel, Sam?" she said, caressing my face with the back of her hand.

I tried to talk, but at first nothing would come out. I swallowed hard.

"My head," was all I could manage to say.

"Yeah, I'll bet," she said, her eyes intensely focused first on one of my eyes and then the other.

Just then the door opened again and a man in a white lab coat walked in and stood by Tracey.

"Mr. McKall, I am Dr. Kent," he said as he grabbed my wrist to take a pulse. "Do you know where you are?"

"A hospital," I forced out.

"That's right. Do you know how you came to be here?" he asked, looking into my face for the first time.

"I'm not sure," I said. "My head hurts."

"Yes, I can imagine it does, Mr. McKall. Your head is going to hurt for some time, I'm afraid. Do you remember anything about the . . . the accident?"

I was confused; I could not really even concentrate on what he was saying, and the question seemed incredibly difficult.

"Can you remember anything about an explosion? Anything at all?" he said.

"I am not sure," was the only answer that seemed to make sense to me as the darkness began to gather in.

The next time I awoke, I saw Tracey was sitting in front of me, but she did not notice that I had woken up. My mind was clearer, and although I could still feel my head throbbing, it did not hurt quite as bad as before. My mouth was as dry as it had ever been and I felt my ankle throbbing as well.

"He's awake." It was Leland's voice; I had not noticed him sitting next to Tracey.

Once again Tracey left the room to get the doctor.

"I need some water," I said to Leland, my lips cracking as I formed the words. He relayed the message to Tracey who relayed it to the nurse.

"What's going on, Leland?" I said.

"Somebody bombed the Fish and Wildlife office. I guess you got hit with some of the debris," he said.

Before he could say anything else, Tracey and the doctor were by my side, Tracey was caressing my face again as Dr. Kent looked into my eyes with a small flashlight. I was thinking about what Leland had said. I had no memory of it whatsoever. In fact, I wasn't even sure how I had gotten to Red Creek.

"What happened?" I said to Leland even though Dr. Kent was standing between Leland and me.

"I was hoping you would know something," Leland said.

"I doubt Mr. McKall can remember anything about the accident, sheriff," said Dr. Kent without taking his eyes off me. "Can you, Sam?"

"Not really," I said.

"Some of it may or may not come back to you," Dr. Kent said. "But you took a pretty serious blow to your head. I put in twenty-three stitches." He held up a mirror to my face. There was a bandage, which centered around the hairline above my right eye.

"You also sprained your right ankle. All the X rays on that were negative. And even though it probably doesn't feel like it right now, you're going to be fine," he said.

"How long am I going to be in here?" I said.

"I want to watch you for another day or so, but if everything goes all right you'll be out of here by tomorrow evening."

Dr. Kent and a nurse spent the next few minutes taking my temperature, blood pressure, and other vital signs. I answered questions about my medical history and signed some forms. Finally, they finished and left the room.

"I've got to go too, Sam," Leland said. "This bombing has brought a horde of reporters to town. They'll be anxious to know you're awake and doing fine."

"Was anybody else hurt?" I asked.

"Well, son, Larry Klinger was in the building. He's . . . dead," Leland said as he reached over and patted my shoulder. "He was a good man too. I didn't always agree with him on things, but this much I can say, he was always . . . always fair." His voice was cracking.

"Why?" I asked as I felt a tear form in my eye.

"I don't know for sure, but we think someone was trying to stop his biological survey."

I felt a tear roll slowly down my cheek and I took a couple of deep breaths to regain my composure and asked, "Any idea who's behind all this?"

"The bomb site investigators from the state police headquarters say the bomb was not very sophisticated but well made. Kind of a homemade bomb on some sort of timer planted in the computer room. They won't have their final report for another forty-eight hours," Leland explained.

"So the short answer to your question is no," he continued. "I don't have any better ideas now than I had before."

"What about Vernon? Is he still on your list?" Tracey asked the question I wanted answered.

"I think whoever did it was trying to destroy the biological survey data. It may not have been intended to kill Larry. Since we don't know when the bomb was set we don't know who on the list has an alibi. Except for Ty Jones, he's been in my jail since this whole thing started. He may be involved in some kind of a conspiracy, but he didn't plant that bomb."

"If Vernon is involved in this thing," I said, "I don't think he's in it alone."

"A lot of people think the same thing. That Vernon is pulling the strings of people like Ty and others. I just don't believe it," Leland said, but I could tell even he was not sure of his brother's innocence anymore.

"What day is it?" I asked Tracey after Leland had left.

"Wednesday, about nine thirty in the morning," Tracey said, looking at her watch.

"It was nice of you to come down here, Tracey," I said.

"I was glad to. I knew your parents were out of the country and somebody should be here," she said, looking at her feet.

"Thank you," I said. "How is the campaign? What's happening?"

"Your death penalty ad is sure causing a lot of stir. It's the first time I've talked about anything other than the environment in two weeks," she said.

"What did Smitty say?" I asked.

"He says it's the best sign yet that we're panicked," she said. Her eyes were searching mine, begging for reassurance.

"He's right, I guess. But when I panic, I drop the hammer. The death penalty is the most powerful symbol in American politics. The Montgomery campaign has to be reeling. What do the numbers look like?" I said.

"The media has been giving us a beating, but the numbers do look better. Our freefall has stopped and stabilized at about forty-three percent. Montgomery is stuck at about forty or forty-one percent. The rest are undecided," she said.

"Well, it looks like we stopped the bleeding at least and we may even have the slim lead. It's not where I wanted to be with only a week to go, but given everything that has happened, I'll take it," I said. I knew that "undecided voters" usually break against the incumbent, so we were still in trouble, but calming everybody's nerves seemed to be a good idea.

Each passing hour brought new clarity to my mind. I had a pretty serious headache and my ankle seemed more than slightly sprained, but despite it all I felt pretty good. I gradually began remembering what happened the day before the explosion. I could remember everything about my round of golf with Jack Kidrick and dealing with the fallout he had created. I could remember looking through our opposition research books and finding the death penalty stuff. I could remember flying to Red Creek and even having dinner with Larry Klinger, but that is where things started to get fuzzy.

In my mind's eye, I could see Larry sitting across from me eating his dinner. But I could not remember what we talked about. I could sense that the memory was still stored somewhere in my mind, but for some reason, I just could not access it. Since it was pretty clear that I was probably the last person to talk to Larry Klinger, I spent a lot of time racking my brain trying to remember.

By the morning of my second day in Creek County Memorial Hospital, it was pretty clear that I was going to be fine. All the tests looked good and Dr. Kent seemed pleased with my progress. My headache had all but subsided and the large bandage, which had been wrapped around my entire head, was replaced with a smaller one.

"All the national media outlets have reporters in town . . . covering this bombing," Tracey blurted out after Dr. Kent left.

"Well, that can't be good," I said as I released a deep breath.

"Most of them want to talk to you so they can finish their stories and go home," she said.

I had not really thought about it, but I suppose if I had, I would have figured that the national media would show for this one. The story was just too good for them to stay away. Environmentalist murdered, government buildings bombed, powerful U.S. senator at the center of it, and an ever-widening, ever-deepening political scandal. Like wackos to Roswell, the media was drawn to Red Creek. Now I was part of the show.

And the show must go on.

We conducted a small impromptu press conference from my hospital bed. As I had suspected, the bombing had turned our own private nightmare into a national news story. The national media were more interested in the bombing side of the story, while the local reporters asked more questions about the campaign and what effect the murders were having. It was a strange mix of questions. Although I could remember very little, I appeared to be an important witness to a major crime that was providing the seminal issue in a political campaign I was managing. One minute I was talking about what time Larry Klinger left the restaurant and the next I was answering questions about our death penalty ad. Strange indeed.

But the main question everybody wanted to know—and that I could not answer—was why I was walking to Larry's office after I had just had dinner with him. I could not answer that; I had no memory of even leaving the Creek Side Café that evening. Try as I might, I could not come up with a reason for me to be going to meet with Larry again.

I answered all the questions the reporters had. When the last reporter left, it was almost 11:00 A.M.

"I really appreciate you being here to help me, Tracey," I said with a sincere sense of gratitude, "but I would feel better if you were handling things at the campaign."

"Well, I thought I would stay until your parents get here," she said.

"I think Dr. Kent is going to let me out this afternoon. If he does, I am going to get on a plane and fly home. My mother won't fly into Wasatch City until tomorrow afternoon. I promise, I'll rest better knowing you are taking care of things up there," I said.

She thought it over for second and then said, "If you insist," and gave me one of her almost—*almost*—imperceptible winks.

I was dressed in street clothes and sitting on the bed when Dr. Kent came by for his afternoon visit.

"All ready to go?" he said, glancing up from my chart.

"All ready," I said.

"Only one problem," he said. "What if I don't release you?"

"I'm fine, Dr. Kent. Really. I need to get back up to Wasatch City. What do you say?"

He looked at my chart then at me and back at the chart again, playing the sadistic game doctors play.

"I did say you might be able to go home today. Didn't I?" he said with a wry smile.

"Yes, you did," I said.

"Well, everything looks good. I'll have them discharge you ASAP."

I left the hospital knowing I would barely have enough time to pack the things I had left at Leland's apartment and still catch the eight-fifteen flight to Wasatch City. One of Leland's deputies had moved my rental car from the Creek Side to the hospital. I drove as fast as I could to the apartment and started packing, keeping a close eye on the time.

The last thing I packed was my laptop computer, which had been on the kitchen table. My traveling case, which doubled as my briefcase, was in the car. I quickly retrieved it from the car. As I opened the briefcase to put the computer in I noticed a green computer disk which I did not recognize. I fished it out of my bag and read the hand-written label, which read DATA BACKUP.

The sight of the disk jogged my memory. I stared at it for a few seconds and then it all came flooding back to me. This had been the reason I was walking to the Fish and Wildlife office, to give Larry his disk back. I sat on the corner of the bed and relived my conversation with Larry.

I held in my hand the reason for Larry's death—the results of the project to which the last months of Larry's life had been dedicated.

I picked up the phone and called Leland's office.

"Sheriff's office. Dispatcher," said a middle-aged woman.

"This is Sam McKall. Is the sheriff in?"

"No, can I take a message?"

"This is rather urgent. Can he be reached?" I asked.

"I can get him on his radio."

"Good. Tell him I remembered my conversation with Larry Klinger and I'm at his apartment"

"Okay. Hang on."

There was a pause while she relayed the message to Leland over the radio.

"He wants you to stay put, he will be by in about an hour. He made it clear that he does not want you to go anywhere," she said.

"I'll be here," I said and made plans to spend one more night in Red Creek.

About fifteen minutes after my message for Leland, I was sitting on my bed nursing a serious headache, when I heard a knock at my door. The top half of the door was a big window covered by a drape. I could tell by the silhouette that it wasn't Leland, but I could not make out who it was.

"Who is it?" I asked through the door.

"Omar," was the one-word answer. I breathed a little easier and answered the door.

"Hi, Omar, come in," I said with a little surprise in my voice.

"I heard you were out of the hospital, thought I'd come by and check on you," he said. Instead of his normal ponytail, his hair hung loose past his shoulders and around his face. He wore a long overcoat that seemed a little warm for the season.

I offered him a chair then sat back down on the bed where I had been when he knocked.

"So, how do you feel? How's your memory? I'd heard you lost some of it," he asked.

"Yes I did, but it is coming back pretty fast now," I answered.

"I guess you feel lucky you weren't closer when the bomb went off," he said.

"That thought has crossed my mind."

"Yes, I'm sure it has. If only Larry could have shared your luck," he said. But I noticed that he was not looking at me as he spoke. His eyes were darting between the window and me and then landed abruptly on my laptop. No, not my laptop, but on Larry's disk, which I had laid on top of my computer. He recognized it—that much was clear.

To this day, I cannot explain what impulse caused me to react this way, but from my bed I lunged for the disk a split second before Omar could. Omar was standing and I was sitting, but I was still two or three feet closer to the disk.

We both reached the disk at the same time. I was able to grab the disk but lost my balance as I tried to protect it. Omar landed with a breathtaking thud right on top of me, trying with all his might to pry the disk from my hands. He dug his unshaven chin into the back of my neck while he scratched and clawed at the disk. I held the disk between my two palms and my fingers clasped together as if I were earnestly praying. Unable to pry the disk from my hands, he wrapped one arm around my throat squeezing my neck with all his might, his arm shaking under the strain. With the other hand he clawed away the bandage on my forehead. The pain was unbearable but was quickly supplanted by panic. I was desperately struggling for air as the blood from my reopened wound began to run into my eyes.

My arms were pinned under my body where I had put them to protect the disk. I struggled to free one and threw the disk as far away from me as I could.

Omar released his grip on my throat and banged my head against the hardwood floor. I sucked as much air in my lungs as I possibly could. As I struggled to catch my breath,

Omar calmly stood up and dusted himself off as if he had accidentally tripped, paying me not the least bit of attention as he retrieved the disk. Then smoothly and without the slightest bit of hesitation he produced a gun from the pocket of his raincoat.

"Fun's over," he said, as if it had been fun up to this point.

Still struggling to catch my breath, I pushed myself into a sitting position. The front of my shirt was covered with blood and I could barely see through the steady stream of it that was running into my eyes. Standing in front of me was a man whom I barely recognized. His eyes were cold and narrow, his face placid and without emotion of any kind.

He looked at the disk—front and back—then put it in his coat pocket. He stared at me for what seemed like a full minute without saying a word or changing the expression on his face. Then slowly he walked toward me, raising the gun so that it was less than an inch from my face and aimed right at my left eye.

"Have you made any copies of this disk?" he asked.

"No. No, I didn't," I said, almost in tears.

"I don't believe you, Sam," he said as he pushed me backward until my head was caught between the wall and his pistol.

"I just found it fifteen minutes ago. I haven't . . . haven't had time," I muttered as he dug the gun's barrel into my forehead.

He bored the gun into my forehead for a few more seconds, then released his grip, keeping the gun pointed at my head.

"Have a seat in the chair," he said, and pointed to one of the chairs at the kitchen table.

I hesitated for a second as I considered whether I should make a break for the door, which was only a few steps away. But Omar, sensing my plan, made a dramatic show of cocking the pistol. I decided I would live longer—although maybe not much longer—if I took the seat.

My legs and arms were shaking as I made my way to the chair and sat down. Omar worked in silence to duct-tape me to the chair.

"Why are you doing this?" I asked, surprised at how shaky my voice was.

But Omar didn't answer me. He just continued to tape. When I was secured to the chair he reached into a pocket on the inside of his coat and produced what looked like a bomb. He sat on the bed facing me and began pressing buttons on the face of the bomb. His hands moved confidently over the buttons.

"What are you doing, Omar? This is crazy," I said. Again he ignored me.

After a few seconds he approached me again and taped the activated bomb to my chest. I felt as though my heart would explode well before the bomb, as Omar taped my mouth closed, took my laptop, turned out all the lights, and left me alone in the dark with his bomb.

I tried to break or tear the duct tape. I strained against it with all my might, but to no avail. I snatched and jerked against it so hard I fell over and hit my head hard against the floor. I fought hard to remain conscious. My head throbbed. A mixture of sweat and blood ran down my forehead into my eyes, but I remained alert, waiting, and struggling.

Until that moment I had never faced the idea that I would die before old age, but in the darkness I could see the illumination of the bomb's red numbers as they rolled closer and closer toward zero.

I had already lived longer than I expected when I heard footsteps approaching and a knock at the door. I was trying to make as much noise as I could so that the person—

whoever it was—would come in. But I was secured so tightly to the chair I was unable to make any noise. Desperately I clenched my fist and tried to yell through my gag, but I knew whoever was at the door would never hear me.

"Sam, are you in there?" It was Leland's voice.

He tried the door but it was locked. I was panicked thinking he would leave, but within a second or two I heard the jangling of keys. Momentarily, he slipped a key into the lock and unlocked it.

Slowly the door opened and Leland stuck his head in to look around. It was dark in the house but the open door allowed in a stream of light from a nearby street lamp, which fell on me like a spotlight. There was a mixture of fear and surprise in Leland's eyes as he hurried to my side and tried to lift me into a sitting position. At first, he must not have noticed the bomb, because he seemed more intent on getting me up and comfortable than dealing with the bomb strapped to my chest.

"Mercy, Sam, are you okay?" he said.

He struggled with his one good arm to get me and the chair upright, and I struggled against him trying to draw attention to the ticking bomb. Finally, he noticed the bomb strapped to my chest.

He dropped me back to the floor and reached into his pocket and produced a small penknife and worked furiously to cut the bomb free. When the bomb fell free and landed with a thud on the floor, I could see that there were only three seconds left on the timer. Still taped to the chair and unable to move, I had never felt so helpless. Leland dropped the knife, grabbed the bomb, and threw it through the front window.

The explosion blew out the rest of the windows in the front of the house and knocked Leland over on top of me in a hail of glass and wood splinters.

I am not sure if Leland was knocked unconscious or not but he lay on top of me without moving for a few seconds. When he came to, he removed the tape from my mouth so that I could talk as he removed the rest of the tape.

"Who did this?"

"Omar Blackford."

"Oh, come on. Omar?" Leland said, stopping to look in my eyes.

"Omar. Said you sent him," I said, my voice still shaking. But I felt the fear begin to subside as anger rose.

"I haven't talked to him since yesterday," he said as he cut my hands free and began to work on my legs.

"I . . . I called your office to tell you I had my memory back and ten minutes later he was knocking on my door."

Leland handed me a handkerchief to wipe the blood from my face.

"He probably picked it up off his police scanner. What did he want?"

"He wanted the computer disk," I was stammering.

"A computer disk?"

"Yeah. When Larry left me at the Creek Side the other night, he accidentally left a computer disk. I think it was the backup disk for the data on his biological survey. That's the way it was labeled, anyway. I was taking it back to him when the bomb went off. I found it when I got back here tonight and then I remembered it all."

"How did he know about the disk? The message I got didn't have anything to do with a disk," Leland said.

"I don't think he came here for the disk. At first he acted like he didn't know what he wanted, but when he saw the disk he was through talking. We fought for a few minutes, but he had a gun. Two minutes later he was gone with the disk and I was taped to this chair with a bomb hanging from my chest. Never even said another word."

"What do you make of it?" Leland asked as I heard sirens approaching.

"I think Omar knew about the disk, even before he set the first bomb. Larry told me that Omar had been helping with the report. When he went to set the bomb, he probably looked for the disk but couldn't find it."

"But what is on that disk that Omar would kill for?" Leland asked more of himself than of me.

"At dinner that night Larry said a lot of people back east would like the results of the survey and that a lot of people back east were going to be very disappointed. But that is not really anything surprising," I said, trying to be helpful.

"Back east?" he said.

"Yeah, back east," I confirmed.

There was a long pause as Leland starred off into the distance—I could tell the wheels were spinning in his head. Momentarily his eyes focused on me and a smile crept onto his face.

"Suppose by back east he means environmentalists. What else could it mean? And what would make them mad?" he said.

"I don't know. What?" I asked.

"I think the data either showed that the yellow-backed minnow was not endangered or at least was inconclusive. That's the only thing that would make them mad. And if I know Omar it would make him mad too. But mad enough to commit cold-blooded murder?" Leland asked trying to come to grips with the situation.

"It's certainly hard to believe. But one thing can't be denied—Larry Klinger is dead and I wasn't far behind when you showed up," I said.

"Once he had the disk, you were the only remaining loose end," Leland said, causing a chill to shoot up my spine.

Within a few minutes the house was full of paramedics, deputies, and worried neighbors. Leland conferred with his deputies while the paramedics attended to my forehead.

I overheard Leland asking one of the paramedics to radio back that there appeared to be no survivors of the explosion. The paramedic who looked to be in his late forties looked confused, but did as he was asked. Leland walked over to check on me.

"What did you do that for?" I asked before he had a chance to say anything.

"What?" he said, unaware that I had overheard him.

"Have him radio that message sent back," I said.

"Oh, that. So Omar will be relaxed, thinking your dead, rather than knowing he's wanted for murder," Leland said. "We're going out to pick him up right now. I'll meet you back at the hospital."

"I'm not going back to the hospital," I said. But Leland didn't hear me, he was already headed for his car. I followed him out and got into the backseat as he and one of his deputies got in the front seat.

"What are you doing?" Leland said.

"I'm going with you," I said as matter-of-factly as I could.

He looked at me for a few seconds through the rearview mirror before saying, "All right, Sam, but you are not getting out of this car. Understand?"

I did.

Chapter Twenty

The drive to Omar's was almost surreal. I have never seen Leland in that state of mind. All I could see of his face were his eyes, which were framed perfectly in the rearview mirror. Whatever doubts and denials Leland had felt back at the house had quickly subsided and had now been replaced with determination. He sat silent in the front seat staring at the darkness in front of the headlights. His deputy sat in the front passenger seat and seemed to be in the same state of mind.

As we drove out of the city limits toward Omar's house I became aware of my surroundings in the way you do the first time you visit a new place or return after a prolonged absence. The night was the first cool night of autumn and the moonless sky was nevertheless clear and bright with stars.

I thought back to my last conversation with Smitty. I don't know how, but somehow he had managed to figure this whole thing out. That was what he was trying to tell

me. I had always assumed that ranchers were the only people with the motive to kill Tate. Smitty had taken another
step further back than I had and seen that Omar also had
a motive: power and prestige. Tate was getting all the
credit, all the attention. It was his picture on the cover of
magazines, it was Tate who appeared on the TV talk shows,
and it was Tate whom the newspapers always quoted.
Smitty in his usual way had seen through the obvious and
recognized the obscure but relevant.

Finally Leland spoke to the deputy. "I'm going to drop
you off where his driveway meets the road, and give you
time to circle around to the back of Omar's house. I'll
knock on his door and arrest him. If there is any trouble
. . . well, you know what to do."

The deputy gave one determined nod, removed his pistol
from its holster, and seemed to give it some kind of in-
spection. He reholstered the gun and folded his arms over
his chest, again resuming his staring.

Within a few minutes we were at Omar's driveway and
Leland had stopped far enough away from the road that
there was no chance Omar could have seen him from his
house even if he had been looking.

Leland and I waited for at least ten minutes for the deputy to get in place before slowly driving up to Omar's front
door. I was thinking that it might be better for him to approach the house more quickly, but did not dare open my
mouth with a suggestion like that. I simply sat in the back
and watched the scene unfold in front of me.

Leland parked the car twenty or thirty yards from Omar's
front door, then he too inspected his gun, opened the door,
and turned to get out of the car. He was almost halfway
out of the car when he stopped and spoke to me for the
first time since leaving the apartment.

"Under no conditions do you get out of this car. If any
thing happens use the radio to call for help," he said.

I nodded vigorously to indicate that I fully intended to comply.

There was only one light on in the front of Omar's house. The large trees that surrounded the house and driveway blocked out most of the stars' light, leaving Omar's house—at least the exterior—dark and foreboding. Leland walked toward the front door with his pistol drawn but hanging by his side in such a way that in the dark of night it would have been very hard to see.

He made it to the house and was about to knock on the door when something caught his attention coming from the garage side of the house. At first I could not see what it was but I saw a look of concern—almost fear—come to Leland's face.

Within a few seconds Leland's deputy stepped into the light that shined on the porch, followed very closely by Omar who was holding a gun to the back of the deputy's head. Omar's face carried the same emotionless expression I had seen less than an hour before.

There was a brief conversation between Leland and Omar which I could not hear but which resulted in Leland bending over and dropping his pistol on the porch. Then slowly backing away with his one good arm raised high above his head and his other half-arm raised to about shoulder height. Turning away from Omar, Leland turned awkwardly and laid face down on the porch.

Likewise, Omar forced the deputy to the ground. Using duct tape, he taped the deputy's hands and feet together behind his back, making it impossible for the deputy to stand or even roll on to his back, and then he turned his attention to Leland.

He was very apprehensive about approaching Leland and kept his gun trained on his head the entire time. I could faintly hear him telling Leland over and over again not to move. Using the deputy's handcuffs, Omar cuffed Leland's one good hand to his belt and then used duct tape to secure both of his arms to his body, finally taping his feet together so that Leland too was incapacitated.

As Omar was taping Leland's arms down I realized that I had wasted at least two or three minutes by not calling for help on the radio. Until now I was too scared to move and even now I was not sure if I could. From time to time Omar would give a nervous look around his yard; each time, his eyes lingered on the car. I sat perfectly still and hid as best I could behind the headrest of the car.

It seemed clear that Omar would kill Leland and the deputy and I had wasted what little time I had cowering in the backseat. Now was the time to move, while Omar was preoccupied with Leland. As quickly as I could I slid from the backseat over the front seat much in the way a snake would have done it—keeping myself as close to the seat as possible.

I was now lying in the front seat, sweat running into my newly opened head wound. I lifted my head up far enough to see between the steering wheel and the dashboard. Omar was dragging Leland and the deputy from the porch to the gravel driveway.

As I fumbled around in the darkness to find the radio, I found a gun stuffed in the crack between the driver's seat and console. I had never held a gun in my hand, much less ever fired a gun. I was surprised by its weight and how comfortably it fit into my hand. I placed the gun under my stomach on the seat and continued my frantic search for the radio mike.

I looked up just in time to see Omar finish dragging the deputy and head back to get Leland. I was not sure what he planning, but I was sure there was no time to wait for backup to arrive. I abandoned my search for the radio and retrieved the gun from the seat.

I rolled down the car window farthest away from the house, crawled out, landing in the damp grass which abutted the gravel driveway, and made my way to the front of the car where I could once again see what was going on.

Omar was standing over Leland and the deputy, his long hair obscuring his face from my view. Seconds passed and I wished that I had not given up my search for the radio mike. In my right hand I tightened my grip on the gun which I was not sure how to aim or fire.

Without any further warning Omar slowly raised his gun taking point-blank aim at Leland's head. My heart was pounding so hard it hurt, I couldn't think clearly. Suddenly I realized I was standing behind the car, pulling the trigger of the pistol which was pointed in Omar's direction.

Nothing happened. Nothing.

I could not budge the trigger. I squeezed with all my might. Nothing. Time was running out. I yelled, "No, Omar!" and ducked again behind the car. I could not see his reaction, but I could hear his slow, deliberate footsteps on the loose gravel as he made his way to the car.

Then a thought hit me. The gun's safety must be on. Although the stars were bright it was not enough to see the gun in any detail. I felt up and down the barrel and handle of the gun to find a switch.

The steps were close now. Frantically I searched the gun.

I found a switch, but dropped the gun as I fumbled with it.

I retrieved the gun, changed the position of the switch, and raised it just as Omar stepped around the car. Without thought I fired. The recoil of the gun surprised me as much as the mis-aimed shot surprised Omar, who, I guess, had expected to find me unarmed.

I scrambled behind the trunk of the car and slowly lifted my head to find Omar. He was nowhere in sight. My heart was racing, my hands shaking, sweat running from every pore.

I thought Omar was probably hiding at the other end of the car, but I could not be sure. I looked under the car but could not see his feet. I slowly stood and raised the gun in an attempt to point it at where I thought Omar must have been. My hands were shaking almost uncontrollably.

"Omar, we don't have to do this," I said, startling myself.

Just then I heard a noise behind me. I wheeled and fired in the direction from which I had heard the noise. In the same instant Omar—who had worked his way around behind me—fired. The bullet flew past my ear and into the rear window of the car. I dove around to the side of the car where I was best shielded from Omar and peeked back to where the shot had come from. I caught a glimpse of Omar taking aim and pulling his trigger. For just a second I felt relief as I realized the shot was not aimed at me. But relief was quickly subsumed by panic when I realized that he was aiming for the gas tank of the car. I dove as far away from the car as I could just as the explosion ripped through the air. I covered my head with my arms as I felt the heat from the explosion engulf me. A split second later bits and pieces of the car were landing all around me in a hail of debris. The hair on the back of my head was singed and my shirt was smoldering. I made two quick rolls to put the fire out and desperately I began to crawl toward the house, staying as far away as I could from Leland and the deputy. When the explosion and its aftermath began to die down I struggled to my feet and made a dash for the house. I had run almost half of the way before Omar noticed me. Bullets began to land all around me. As I ran, I held the gun behind me and squeezed off two rounds without even looking where I was firing.

Suddenly, I felt a sharp burning pain rip through my left shoulder. The impact knocked me to the ground. The pain was unlike anything I had ever felt. I could not move my arm; there was blood everywhere. Somehow I managed to keep my wits about me. Sitting on my knees, I used my one good hand to search for the gun. Again I heard the crunching of Omar's deliberate footsteps—I knew any second he would be standing over me, finishing the job.

I found the gun just in time to see Omar standing over me and raising his gun.

Without even a moment's hesitation, I raised my gun and fired.

Chapter Twenty-one

I guess Smitty really summed it up best in two articles published in the *Capitol Times* the week after the election. The first appeared the morning after the election.

Utah voters took a long look at the tenure of Senator Margaret Hansen this fall and despite some obvious concerns, punched her ticket for another six-year term in the world's most exclusive club: the United States Senate.

Hansen eked out a narrow victory against the hard-charging former U.S. attorney Jeff Montgomery, who campaigned against his opponent's environmental record and lengthy tenure in the U.S. Senate.

Montgomery's campaign had been helped by the recent murder of prominent environmentalist Steve Tate, a longtime political foe of Hansen.

"There is no question that the murder played a significant role in this campaign. Without it we never would have come this close," said one Montgomery campaign insider.

"The whole thing was very strange," he added.

Many had believed that Tate was murdered by a cattle rancher and a significant portion of that suspicion had been directed at Vernon Hansen, a brother of Senator Hansen. Vernon has since been cleared and authorities now believe that Tate and U.S. Fish and Wildlife agent Larry Klinger, who was killed in a subsequent bombing, were both murdered by Omar Blackford, the venerated father of the Red Creek environmental movement.

"This has been the toughest and most personally painful election I've ever had. But I can tell you I will be a stronger and better senator because of it," said Hansen to a packed house of visibly relieved supporters. . . .

Later that same week came this story, which appeared on the Op-ed page:

THE RED ROCK CREEK MURDERS

Bizarre and tragic do not even begin to describe the recent murders in Red Creek. Although many of the facts surrounding these murders will never be known for sure, authorities in Red Creek have settled on the following theory to explain the crimes.

Until Steve Tate arrived in Red Creek back in 1988, Omar Blackford had been the recognized founder, leader, and front man of the Red Creek environmental movement. Tate, however, was a more flamboyant and dynamic leader than Blackford and when he arrived on the scene much of the limelight was cast on him.

As Blackford was pushed further and further into the background, a jealousy developed. This animosity festered and grew over a matter of years. At some point, no one knows for sure when, Blackford conceived the plan to murder Tate.

His plan was risky and involved framing one of the state's largest cattle ranchers, Vernon Hansen.

Hansen maintains a small fleet of pickup trucks which his ranch hands use. Because these trucks are used on an as needed basis, no one noticed when Blackford stole one from the ranch late in the afternoon of October 8.

Once he had the truck, Blackford drove out to Sidewinder Canyon, and retrieved the .22-caliber rifle which he must have known would be behind the truck's seat. He found Tate and shot him in the back of the head. After the murder Blackford simply returned the stolen truck and murder weapon to Hansen's ranch.

As planned, in the wake of Tate's murder, Blackford was thrust back into the forefront of the yellow-backed minnow controversy. Once again he was at the head of the movement he had fathered.

There was one more problem for which Blackford had not planned. The U.S. Fish and Wildlife Service had been performing a month-long biological survey designed to determine if the yellow-backed minnow was a candidate for the Endangered Species List. The long-awaited test results, which were to provide scientific basis for listing, were inconclusive. Blackford, who had developed a close working relationship with U.S. Fish and Wildlife officer Larry Klinger, somehow received advance notice of the results.

Blackford knew that everything he had worked for, even murdered for, rested on that research conclusively proving that the yellow-backed minnow was headed for extinction. The data was to provide the linchpin. But since that was not to be the case, Blackford decided that it too had to be destroyed; perhaps thinking that this would force a new study.

It is not clear if Blackford planned to murder Klinger or not, but in any case, sometime on the afternoon of October 15 Blackford planted a bomb in the computer room of the U.S. Fish and Wildlife office. A place he knew all the research data was stored.

At 6:53 that evening, the bomb went off, killing Klinger, wounding Sam McKall and destroying what Blackford thought was the only copy of the data.

Ironically, if he had set the bomb detonation time for a few minutes later, he might have succeeded in his plan. But that was not to be.

In a twist of fate which no one could have anticipated, earlier that evening Klinger had had dinner with McKall and inadvertently left behind a computer disk containing his backup copy of the all the test data. . . .

The article continued the sequence of events I knew all too well. I read Smith's and the rest of the paper while enjoying my morning coffee at my usual coffeehouse. The story that he pieced together seemed plausible enough. But it didn't tie up all the loose ends. Some people thought that the Blackford plan to kill Steve began back when Ty Jones was caught with a bomb and was widely believed to have made threats against Tate. Indeed the state crime lab had determined that the bomb taken from Ty on the occasion was the same type Blackford used at the U.S. Fish and Wildlife office, and the one used against me.

And there are those who continue to believe that there were two murderers, who killed Steve Tate, and Omar, who killed Klinger. They argue that these crimes were to-

Eric C. Evans

tally separate and that Steve's murderer has gotten away with it. Like Smitty, I don't believe it.

My arm was still in a sling, but after five days in the hospital the doctors assur[ed] me that my shoulder would completely heal. I took a leisurely walk back to my apartment, thinking about all I ha[d b]een through in the last month.

There are certain thin[gs] you never consider happening to you. And being sucked [into] a murder investigation, becoming a potential victim, a[nd ki]lling the murderer only a split second before he could [kill y]ou is not one of them.

They gave me credit [for s]olving the Tate and Klinger murders, when in reality [nothi]ng could be farther from the truth. I just happened to [have the] ringside seats. I never suspected Omar, not until he [showe]d up on my doorstep with a gun and a bomb, and it [was ju]st shear dumb luck that I was in the back of Leland'[s tha]t shear dumb luck that I there and seriously wounde[d] [O]mar's hand twice; still I did not feel comfortable with [the] attention I was getting.

I spent the last week of th[e camp]aign in the hospital. I had done what I could from [there] but for the most part Tracey had taken over and do[ne an ex]cellent job. The final days of almost all campaigns [are noth]ing more than confusion. You can imagine how [the fan]atics around these murders only made it worse. B[ut] [a]nd confusion normally is an ally of the status qu[o] [in] this case Maggie represented the status quo.

Elections are great endings an[d] [beg]innings. That is one of the great things about p[olitics] [the] end of every campaign—win or lose—provide[s an] [o]pportunity for a new beginning.

I found Maggie working at her [office in] the Federal Building.

"You got a minute?" I said, stic[king my hea]d into her office as casually as I could.

"Yes. Certainly, come in," she said.

"I have something I want you to read," I said as I handed her a letter and sat in one of the two soft leather chairs in front of her desk.

Maggie read for a second, lifted her eyebrows as if she was surprised, but I knew she really wasn't. She dutifully finished the whole letter then looked up at me.

"You're sure about this?" she asked, looking at me over her reading glasses.

"I think I am," I said, nodding my head as if I were still trying to convince myself.

"What are your plans?"

"I don't really have any just yet." I knew Maggie would not like that—she always had a plan. "I am going to take some time off, spend some time rehabbing my arm, do some travelling," I said, trying to make it sound like an actual plan.

There was an awkward pause, neither of us knowing what to say.

"I am going to miss you, Sam," Maggie finally said. "I have always trusted your judgment completely. I could never ask someone to do for me what you have done over the last month. It will be hard to replace someone like that."

I had had enough adulation, so I changed the subject.

"This is a little awkward, but I think you should replace me with Tracey. She's the best person you've got."

"That is an intriguing idea," Maggie said as the smile of a Cheshire cat crept onto her face.

Tracey was cleaning out her desk at the campaign office when I walked in.

"How are you, Sam?" she asked. It had been several days since I had seen her.

"Better every day," I said, lifting my wounded arm about chin high to show the improvement.

"What are your plans?" I asked.

"I'm going to take the rest of the month off. Visit my family in Maine. Relax," she said.

"Well, there is one more press release I need you to write before you leave," I said.

"Okay, what is it?" she said as she grabbed a legal pad out of one of her boxes and located a pen.

I gave her a copy of my resignation letter.

"You can't be serious," she said, waiting for the punch line.

"Yes. Yes, I am and I recommended you as my replacement."

"Get out of here. You didn't resign. Not after everything that has happened," she said, leaning back in her chair as if she were out of breath.

"I've done everything I can do here. It is time to move on."

"Well, what are you going to do?"

"I don't know. I'm going to take some time to decide." Tracey, I knew, would understand that answer.

"Judging by Maggie's reaction, I think you've got the inside track to replace me," I said.

"Do you really think so?"

"I do."

"I'd rather have you there, but if you are going to leave . . ." She let her smile finish her thought.

"You'll be great in that job . . . and maybe when I am back in D.C. we can have dinner or something," I said as nonchalantly as I could.

"That would be good." Her response was equally nonchalant but less contrived.

But as I got up to leave, she flashed me a smile and yes, definitely a wink.